MONSTERS IN OUR WAKE

J.H. MONCRIEFF

SEVERED PRESS
HOBART TASMANIA

MONSTERS IN OUR WAKE

ISBN: 978-1-925597-32-5

To Water Protectors everywhere.

CHAPTER ONE

I hadn't seen a person in over seventy years, and that's the way I liked it. People were the nastiest sort of creatures: destructive, messy, irritating. Even though I avoided direct contact with them, evidence of their existence was always creeping into my home, and into the homes of my friends. Thankfully, I had a stronger hold on my temper than most, or they would have had to deal with me long before now.

As much as I didn't want to see people, it would have been much worse for them to see me. Let's just say most of them wouldn't have gotten over it for a long, long time. That's if they survived, which wasn't likely.

We could tell a confrontation was coming. The first clumsy explorations of my home had made me laugh, but I was more concerned than I let on. However, I knew there was no point in panicking. What would be, would be.

The shock waves had been the worst, or so we'd thought. I was awakened by a blast that shook my home to its foundations and made my ears bleed. To say it put me in a bad mood would be an understatement of seismic proportions. My wife had burst into the lair, screaming, but while I could see her mouth moving, I couldn't hear a single word. Her ears were bleeding as well, and watching the dark fluid stream down her cheeks brought an awareness of what was happening to me.

My wife hadn't been the only one screaming. The blue whales shrieked in pain and fear, their navigational bearings disrupted by the aftershocks. They had no idea where they were, poor little things. My wife had put aside her own fear to rush above and comfort them. I stayed below, watching as the very walls shimmered in front of me, wondering what all this meant and what I was going to do about it. We'd had earthquakes before, of course, but nothing like this. This was manmade, and I knew it. I could *smell* it.

Several years had passed since that wretched day, and I had let myself be lulled into complacency. However, if I am to be truly honest, I suppose I never fully left the horror of that moment behind me. I had known all along that something even more terrible was coming—that it was only a matter of time until my family would face a new threat to our way of life.

I rarely rose to the surface. There was no good reason to, and in any case, I loathed the sun. It dried my skin and blinded me. Better to stay in the cold, dark depths where few dared to venture. The other creatures left me alone, and except for taking enough to sustain my family, I left them alone. It was a peaceful arrangement that had worked well for hundreds of years. I saw no reason to alter it.

However, being absent was not the same as being unaware, although I had often wished it were. I was aware of most things that took place on the surface of my ocean, so when the humans began to bring their miserable ships into our territory, no one had to tell me. Their presence was obvious when they were still hundreds of miles away. Their dull minds, their clumsy, awkward movements, the racket they made—just the thought of humans was enough to make me shudder. Clearly, I had stayed below the surface for too long. Not only had the rumors of my kind died out decades before—now my very existence was in doubt. I had become a fictional boogeyman. Which was fine with me, but it was obvious that the humans' ignorance couldn't be allowed to continue. Sooner or later, they were going to discover what they were dealing with.

We are not ignorant creatures. I knew why the humans were stumbling around my territory. I could smell it, you see—the oil that flowed beneath my floor. It had always been there, and as humans took over the world with the tenacity of a virus, I knew they would eventually use their bumbling, inefficient methods to sniff it out for themselves. But I forced this unwelcome thought out of my mind and concentrated on other things, pleasant things, pretending the possibility didn't exist.

I did suggest every millennium or so that we move, but the wife wouldn't hear of it. This was our home, the home of our great and powerful ancestors, and the home of our child. In any case, the cursed fuel was everywhere. And with it came the humans. Any escape we achieved would be temporary at best.

The day the first drill was lowered, I snapped it into several dozen pieces. I must admit I did it without thinking—destroying it required the minutest flexing of my jaws, and I smiled to think of how much I must have just cost them. Any joy I felt was fleeting, though, for I knew they would return. My wife frowned as the shattered pieces drifted down to litter our floor, and when she looked at me, I could see the worry in her eyes.

"What are we going to do?" she asked, and I reassured her as best I could, but the truth was, I had no clue. While I could drift around, snapping drills into pieces all day long, eventually stronger measures would have to be taken. There were many more of them than there were of us, and if our great ancestors had been as wise as everyone claimed, they would have solved the problem long ago instead of occasionally snacking on a few sailors. Even if I tore their precious ship into slivers of metal and ripped each human being upon it apart, I'd only slow the process. Swarms of humans would come, armed with weapons of increasing destruction. And while I wasn't afraid of their little guns and rockets, which were mere fireworks to us, I was concerned for my fellow sea creatures, who would be obliterated in the scuffle.

I laughed at the humans' dismay when they saw their nasty probe turned to scrap metal, and I resolved to do the same to every drill they plunged into my beloved home, be it one or ten or a thousand more. The humans had the gift of plentitude, but I had two things they did not.

Wisdom and patience.

Infinite, infinite patience.

CHAPTER TWO

Flora Duchovney was hiding below deck when she heard the commotion. Of course, she'd never acknowledge she was hiding, just like she'd never confess she still had a problem working for the company. It was hard enough being the only woman on board without admitting to any sensitivity. Sensitivity wasn't popular here; she'd figured that out right away. Along with showing concern for anything but profit, it was cause for immediate derision. Even though she'd theoretically been hired for her geological expertise, she'd learned early on that her opinion wasn't welcome. It was best to keep her mouth shut and look the other way. It was a matter of survival, really. Perhaps when she returned to the mainland, she'd call some journalists and toss them a few tidbits. Nothing that would lead to her, of course, although she was certain the men would instantly know who had betrayed them.

She'd wait until she cashed her check. Zach came first. He always did. The ocean may have been her first love, but Zach was her deepest.

Flora had heard the men sound angry before, of course—the majority of them were *always* angry. It was a lousy job, and while it paid well, the knowledge that you were making ungrateful people rich was a tough pill to swallow. In that one small way, she understood them.

This time, however, was different. The men were shouting at each other, and the language was enough to turn the air blue. What if something was wrong with the barge? She hadn't felt anything out of the ordinary, but what if they were sinking? They were in the middle of the South Pacific, with nothing but cerulean water stretching in every direction. If they sank, she'd never see Zach again. The thought hastened her footsteps as she hurried up the stairs.

"What is it? What's wrong?"

The captain turned on her, his face a florid red that warned of hypertension. He'd be dead in a few years if he wasn't careful, but the knowledge brought only temporary comfort. "I thought you said the path was clear. I thought you said there were no obstructions." As he screamed at her, flecks of his spittle struck her face. She resisted the urge to wipe them away.

"It was. It is," she said, feeling at a loss. The men glared at her. She took an unsteady step toward the cabins. "What happened?"

"What *happened* is you don't know shit. There *is* an obstruction, and since you can't tell your ass from the ocean, we've just lost millions. Not to mention several days' time."

"I assure you, Captain—there was no obstruction. My surveying was accurate. The information I gave you was correct." Flora could hear the waver in her voice, and she forced herself to straighten her shoulders and rise to her full height, which wasn't much compared to the rest of the crew. She couldn't weaken in front of these goons. No matter what happened, they must never suspect they'd gotten to her.

"Then how do you explain *this*?" Apostolos thrust a piece of jagged metal at her—metal that dripped with seawater, enhancing the strong metallic smell. She had no idea what it was, but she retreated another step, proud she hadn't flinched when he'd flung whatever it was at her face.

"I—I wish I could. Can someone please tell me what's going on?" She glanced around the group, but didn't find a single ally. The eyes that glared at her were unanimously cold. Every face was sunburned and windburned a dusky red, and none were clean-shaven. Men discarded such niceties very quickly when they were miles away from civilization. She thought of *Lord of the Flies* and suppressed a shudder.

Finally, a voice of reason chimed in. "That's what's left of our drill, Ms. Duchovney. We hit something." His name was Tim—or maybe Todd? She couldn't remember. It started with a *T*, in any case. He looked younger than the rest, and maybe that made him less of a Neanderthal. She could only hope.

"I don't understand. There was nothing to hit. This…this isn't rocket science, gentlemen. We're in the middle of the ocean.

We're too far away from shore for any reef, and the survey was clean. You saw the results."

Apostolos spat and threw the hunk of twisted metal at her feet, making her jump. A few of the men smirked, and she hated them for it. "This is the only result I care about, Ms. *Duchovney*. The rest of it ain't worth shit, and as far as I'm concerned, that includes you."

The captain pushed past her, cursing under his breath, leaving her alone with the rest of the crew.

"Did—did anyone feel it hit anything?" She groped for answers like a blind woman, hoping for a glimmer of something that would make sense. She'd studied the results carefully. There had been no obstruction—she was certain of that. There was nothing below them but clear blue water.

And oil.

Lots and lots of oil.

"Nothing. Everything was going as planned, and then suddenly the drill shattered. You see what's left of it," Tim or Todd said. There couldn't have been more than ten inches.

"But that's impossible. Steel doesn't *shatter*. If you'd hit something, the drill would have stopped. You'd feel the obstruction," Flora said, determined to plead her case even though she knew her words were falling on deaf ears. She couldn't explain what had happened, but she was certain she wasn't to blame. Nothing in the survey could account for this. Actually, nothing in her career could explain it. "Steel doesn't shatter," she repeated.

"I know, but it did. That piece there? That's all we could save of it. I guess the rest is at the bottom of the ocean," Tim/Todd said with a shrug.

"What about sonar? Did anyone check?"

He flushed scarlet. "That would have been the smart thing to do. Unfortunately, we didn't think of it. I know it was clear when we started drilling."

Muttering curses, most of the men headed below deck, no doubt to drink themselves silly.

When they were gone, she retrieved the metal. It was cold and shockingly heavy. What could have destroyed it so thoroughly?

The loss of the drill was a terrible setback. It would take time to construct a new drill string—too much time, and that was only if the necessary materials were on board. Flora knew from her training manual that crews were often prepared to replace segments of the string, but not everything at once. If they had to return to the mainland, more precious days would be wasted. It might be weeks before she was reunited with her son.

She forced the thought out of her mind. She didn't have the luxury of getting upset—at least, not now. Although she was at a loss just as great as anyone else on the ship, she was the best person to formulate the answers.

As she turned the twisted chunk of metal over and over in her hands, she saw what looked like great gouges in the steel. Pulling the fragment closer, she ran her fingers along the deep grooves, cutting herself.

Flora hurried to the side of the boat, sucking the blood from her finger as she studied the ocean. It was deceptively calm, like an endless mirror. She loved days like this, but even they were not to be trusted. The ocean could change in a matter of minutes, crushing small craft before it smoothed out again. An endless cycle of life and death.

How could she tell these men the truth? She couldn't. They wouldn't believe her. Worse, they would laugh at her.

Still, her knowledge of biology had given her the impossible answer. Impossible, but nonetheless real.

Those were tooth marks on the metal. Tooth marks from a creature not yet identified by science. Nothing known could have snapped a solid piece of industrial steel into so many pieces.

There was something out there. Something unknown. Something that could shatter metal with a single bite.

"Where are you?" she whispered as her eyes scanned the ocean. Not a single ripple appeared to answer her, but she felt something had heard her just the same.

Shivering, she rushed to join the men below decks.

She could use a drink.

CHAPTER THREE

The men groaned when they heard her step on the stair. Thor Anderssen couldn't understand why they'd taken such a loathing to the scientist. Having a woman on board was a good thing, as far as he was concerned.

"That's all we need—a bloody fucking chaperone. Maybe she'll scold us for being too loud." Frank said the last two words in a squeaky falsetto, setting off a chorus of guffaws. Thor had noticed the sailor was in a particularly foul mood that day, but then again, they all were. Working on the barge was miserable hard work, and the destruction of the drill string would set them back by at least a week. Most of the men had families at home they were looking forward to seeing, and the delay had made them furious. Thor had no one waiting, which made it a little easier. The only person he could disappoint was himself.

"Take it easy, guys. She's not so bad," he said.

Flora cleared the last step as the words left Thor's mouth. The smile on her face faltered, and he could see her eyes were watery. As shitty as the men were feeling, he knew she must be feeling worse.

He pulled the last chair out from under George's feet. The big man grumbled and swore, but Thor ignored him. George he could handle—he was more snarl than bite, but some of the others he wouldn't mess with.

As she picked her way through the group to take the seat he offered, she looked like a frightened deer with her huge dark eyes. Thor wanted to shake her, to tell her not to act so damned timid and scared all the time. He was sure it was difficult being the only woman on ship, but these guys were animals. Acting like prey was a good way to get yourself killed.

"Would you like a beer?"

He was surprised when she nodded. Every other time they'd knocked back a few, she'd barricaded herself in her cabin. The only private cabin on the ship—not even Apostolos had his own. It was another awesome decision on the part of the company, perfectly maximizing the resentment.

Thor handed her one from his stash.

"Thanks...Todd?"

He grinned. *I wish.* "Thor," he corrected, ignoring the laughter from around the table. He'd heard it before. As her eyes widened, he held out a hand in a futile attempt to hold off the inevitable. "I know, I know. I don't look like a Thor."

Maybe the name had made more sense when he was a kid, when his hair had still been blond, but he'd been bald as a bat when he was born. Perhaps it had been wishful thinking on his parents' part.

"It's not that," she said. "It's just—"

"It's my cross to bear, is what it is. It's actually quite a common Scandinavian name, but then those damn movies had to come out, with that Australian guy."

"Hemsworth," a guy named Liam said. He was a fellow geek, another engineer. Between them, they brought the musculature on board down by several levels. "His name is Chris Hemsworth."

"Whatever." Thor snorted to convey his deep disgust at the thought of an Australian portraying one of the most kickass Nordic gods of all time. "It certainly ain't Thor."

"So, we'll be needing a new survey then, milady?" Apostolos shouted across the table, setting off another batch of groans.

"Not necessarily," Flora said, and Thor choked on his beer.

"What the hell kind of shit are you talking, lady? Your fucking drill site has set us back a week, maybe more. You want we should try it again?" Frank glowered at her in a way that suggested if she'd been a man, she'd already have a black eye. Thor wondered if it was worth sticking his neck out to calm the man down. Frank could break him in half with one fist, but the old sailor seemed to respect him. Most of the time.

"The site is fine." Flora cleared her throat and looked around the table. "There is no obstruction. Nothing permanent, anyway. But we still might want to move on."

Thor jumped in before the others could ask the question in a less civilized manner. "I don't understand. What do you mean, there isn't an obstruction? What did we hit?"

Flora sighed. "We didn't hit anything. Something hit us." She withdrew the metal from her pocket. Frank growled when he saw the remains of the drill string. No one would miss that her hands were trembling, but Thor was relieved she'd found her voice.

She passed the bit of drill string to him. "See those markings right there?" She pointed to some deep grooves in the metal with a fingertip. He held the metal to the light. The indentations were like nothing he'd ever seen before. But he guessed that wasn't that surprising, since he'd never seen steel shatter like glass, either.

"Yeah," he said, returning it to her. "What about it?"

Flora hesitated, biting her lip. She glanced around the table again. "They're tooth marks."

The table erupted—everyone but Thor jumped at the chance to jeer at her. Flora looked frightened, but to her credit, she squared her shoulders and waited. It took several long minutes before Frank's voice could be heard above the din.

"Are you trying to tell us—?" The sailor choked on a laugh before he could finish. "Are you actually trying to tell us there's a bloody *sea monster* down there?"

Flora's face turned almost as red as Frank's. "I'm not saying it's a sea monster, but it's some kind of creature, yes."

"Could be a shark," Liam said, sounding hopeful. Thor was relieved at least one of the guys was being reasonable.

She shook her head. "No shark has this kind of power, or teeth this large. At least, not one we've identified."

"Ooooh, beware the mystical giant shark. It's coming to get us. There it is now." Frank waggled his fingers on top of his head to simulate a shark's fin, while the other men sang the *Jaws* theme with varying skill. Apostolos was one of the only ones not laughing. Thor had yet to see him crack a smile.

"Maybe it's something like Megalodon. It's happened before, where people have discovered living creatures once believed to be extinct," Thor said.

Frank rolled his eyes. "Yeah, and maybe it's a giant squid."

"Giant squids don't have teeth, you dumbass."

"Sure they do. And who are you calling a dumbass, dumbass?"

Flora slammed her beer down hard enough to make it foam out the top. She pushed her chair away from the table and stood, hands on her hips, eyes narrowed. "I should have known you weren't mature enough to deal with this. You're no better than a bunch of children."

It was difficult to make a dramatic exit in such cramped quarters, but she did her best. Soon enough the men heard the slamming of her cabin door, followed by the click of the lock. The crew laughed harder.

"Aren't you going to run after your girlfriend, mate?" Frank's eyes glittered with hilarity and booze. If he wanted to get a rise out of Thor, he'd picked the wrong guy. Thor had three younger sisters—Frank was welcome to do his worst. "It's fucking obvious you've got a thing for her."

Thor finished his beer. "Nah, I'm not in the mood tonight."

As his inane joke earned more laughs, he felt guilty. Flora was only trying to do her job. She didn't deserve to be mocked and ridiculed because she didn't piss standing up. He wondered if she'd had any idea what she was in for when she agreed to be their surveyor.

"Dumb fucking broad," Apostolos said once it was quiet again. "Nothing but dead weight. Blaming her incompetence on sea monsters. And I thought I'd seen everything." He spat into the red bandanna he carried with him before tucking it into his pocket. Thor sincerely hoped he didn't make his wife wash that thing. "Next she'll be saying fucking unicorns did it. Soon as we get to shore, I'm letting her go."

Apostolos was infamous for hating the men who worked under him, but at least he loathed everyone equally. The only way to tell he approved of someone's work was if he asked him to join another of his crews. This was Thor's third job with Apostolos, so he hoped that meant he was standing on a sturdier deck than most.

Thor examined the scarred piece of metal Flora had left behind. "These do look like tooth marks." He tossed the bit of steel to the captain. "And I've never seen a creature that could do this kind of damage. She didn't say it was a sea monster. She said she didn't know *what* it was."

Apostolos slammed the metal down on the table with a thud. "Pah. They're dents. They don't look like tooth marks to me. For all we know, she's making this shit up as she goes along. My decision is final. She's done."

The captain folded his arms, signaling the subject was closed, but Thor knew Flora had a marine biology background—geology had only been her minor. If anyone on the crew could tell the difference between tooth marks and plain old dents, it was her.

As much as he wanted Apostolos to reconsider—there had to be some reason a scientist like Flora had taken this job, and he suspected the reason was money—Thor also hoped she was wrong.

An obstruction they could deal with. But a creature capable of reducing solid steel to rubble?

If it could do that to the drill, what could it do to them?

CHAPTER FOUR

"What are we going to do about them, Nøkken?"

My wife tore around our home, destroying knickknacks and priceless treasures with each thrash of her tail. When she crushed our son's shipwreck collection, I realized I had to do something to calm her before she did the humans' work for them.

Stretching myself to full size, I moved to block her, hoping the sight of someone she loved would make her stop. The female of our species is larger, stronger, and much more deadly. They've been known to reduce their entire family to chum in a single fit of temper. It's not surprising the males are taught to respect and obey them from birth.

The risk I took was huge, but we'd been happily married for over five thousand years. Surely that counted for something.

When she saw me blocking her path, her eyes narrowed. I prepared to defend myself, as futile as that would be. She glided toward me until our snouts were nearly touching.

"Let. Me. *Pass*."

"Darling, you must calm down. They are vermin. Barnacles on our backsides. It's not worth getting yourself into a lather over. I can take care of them, I promise."

I believed I already had, by destroying that child's toy they'd dared to plunge into our home. At least temporarily. We both knew they'd return. Such is the way with vermin.

"You don't have the spine for it." She snarled at me, showing off needle-sharp fangs dripping with ichor. This was *not* going to be a good day. "You've always been too soft-hearted, Nøkken. We see evidence of their destruction every single day, and yet you insist on letting them live." She pushed by me with the slightest flick of her tail, and I went crashing into the wall, badly torn by her scales. A school of tuna appeared, darting this way and that, most likely drawn by the odor of my blood. I ate a few, but they were so puny I could barely feel their tiny bones crunch between my teeth. It didn't help.

"I will *rend* them," my wife screamed, and propelled herself to the surface as if an irresistible force had launched her. Sighing, I shook my head, but I wasn't worried. I knew she'd turn away before the humans saw her. In spite of her inconvenient temper, Draugen was no fool.

The sad story of our distant cousin Uisge served as a cautionary tale. A single peek at the world above her beloved loch, and she'd become a reluctant celebrity. Now humans constantly invaded her home with their cameras and ridiculous sonar equipment, eagerly anticipating the next sighting. Poor Uisge. The lady gets no peace, despite having stayed well hidden for decades. Whenever we hear from her, she is understandably depressed.

"I would have torn them apart. All of them, until there was not a single one left to snap a picture," Draugen always vowed, cursing her cousin for being weak and stupid and softhearted. Unfortunately, Uisge's window of opportunity was barred shut. The one time violence would have done some good was in 1933. But how could she have anticipated what would happen? Humans used to fear us. Now they sought us out.

Our long lives have provided us with many benefits, including the opportunity to witness evolution at work. We've watched creatures become stronger, more agile, and less vulnerable with time. Those who don't adapt die out, and that is something we've been forced to accept. But the great mystery is how human beings have evolved backward, becoming less intelligent with every generation. In spite of this, they continued to propagate at an alarming rate.

It boggled the mind.

When they first arrived on the scene, they were comical creatures, really. Stumbling around, grunting and snorting, barely able to feed themselves. And the *smell*. I hate to be boorish, but it was enough to knock you over. They were clearly kissing cousins with the apes, but at least the apes were civilized. Apes knew how to keep themselves clean, something early man obviously hadn't discovered.

"Well, this won't last long," I said to my wife, and we shared a good laugh over it. But now I feared the humans would be the ones laughing last. And if that was the case, we could bid goodbye to this great earth and every living being upon it.

The cave-dwelling years, known to our kind as the "good old days," didn't last long. This new creature was possessed with an uncontrollable desire to explore, to reach, to expand its boundaries. Wherever it went, it was hell-bent on destruction. Wild spaces, other organisms—even those of its own kind—met death at its hands. While watching humans used to be a mindless form of entertainment, the wife and I grew worried as we saw these crude monsters destroy each other. We'd never seen another animal act this way, before or since. Humans appeared to be on a brutal quest for power, a thirst that was never quenched or even slackened. We buried our heads in our beloved ocean, thankful we didn't have to deal with them—a virtue of being able to avoid dry land entirely.

We should have known what was coming.

By the time they'd perfected sea travel—well, perfected it as much as they could ever hope to—we knew not to snicker at their tiny boats, which resembled so many toys scattered across the great roof of our home. A creature that has no consideration for its own kind is one that needs to be regarded with caution.

As they discovered what the ocean had to offer, it was inevitable that more and more humans would take to the water. For the first time in our history, man was in our territory. It was inevitable that we'd have skirmishes.

The old men of the sea were more intelligent than I'd given them credit for. Instead of charging us with their primitive weapons, which I'd seen them do to other beasts, they screamed in terror at a mere glimpse of me or my wife, and struggled to steer their tiny craft in the other direction. My son loved to play with shipwrecks, and collected them like treasure. In more than a few of the relics, he'd found some old maps with our territory circled in faded ink. The maps were too miniscule for us to read, so we relied upon him to tell us what they said. As much as we loathed the humans, we were always curious to discover what crazy invention they'd think of next.

Here be dragons, the seamen had written, and it made my wife smile. Before long, the sailors had found another route to travel between their beloved Europe and the so-called New World, and we were left in peace.

It's a pity things always have to change.

CHAPTER FIVE

Flora didn't sleep that night. Her claustrophobia had returned with a vengeance, and she spent the hours until dawn staring at the bunk above her, feeling like the weight of the ocean was pressing down on her chest, crushing her. The sedative her doctor had given her for such moments failed to kick in. Sometimes, she suspected he'd humored her tales of crippling anxiety and panic attacks by giving her a placebo. Her friend Meredith, a psychiatric nurse, had assured her the pills were the real deal.

Fat lot of good they were doing her now.

She knew all the tricks. She raised her arms over her head to get more air into her lungs. She turned her head to the side so she was staring into her tiny room instead of at the upper bunk, which was much too close to the tip of her nose. She took deep, slow breaths to prevent hyperventilation.

And still her mind betrayed her.

You can't breathe. You're going to die. You can't breathe. You must get out. Can't breathe. Going to die. Must get out. Must get OUT.

Can'tbreathedyingcan'tbreathegetoutgetoutgetout.

The psychiatrist had taken her more seriously than the doctor had, but she'd only been able to see him three times before her coverage ran out. Three fifty-minute sessions didn't even crack the surface of everything that was wrong with her. Thankfully, along with the tricks he'd given her one crucial piece of information.

"When you're claustrophobic, your body sends a fight-or-flight signal to your brain. That's why you feel like you're dying. But if you wait it out, your body will send another signal that lets the brain know the danger has passed. All you have to do is wait."

"Wait?" The idea of experiencing a panic attack for longer than a minute was terrifying. "For how long?"

"It varies, but typically, twenty minutes should do it," the psychiatrist said in the matter-of-fact manner of someone who had never suffered from clinical anxiety.

Twenty minutes. Just twenty minutes.

But hadn't it already been hours? It certainly felt that way.

When the tricks didn't work and even the sedative failed, she whispered to herself. "You're okay, Flora, you're fine. You're in your cabin and you're safe and nothing's going to happen to you."

She forced herself not to think of the shattered drill string or the teeth marks.

She tried not to think at all.

Flora didn't know why she bothered whispering. She could have shouted show tunes at the top of her lungs and still gone unheard. From their boisterous discussion in the messdeck, the men either thought she was still awake—or they didn't care.

She heard Apostolos broach the possibility of returning to the mainland. She also heard him vow to fire her the second the ship docked. Before she could pull her pillow over her ears, Thor had defended her, trying to reason with them, and for a moment, she felt hopeful. But the rest of the guys only mocked him.

Unfortunately, she heard that too.

The one benefit of insomnia was that it gave a person plenty of time to think, and at about three in the morning, Flora felt she'd devised a solution. Even though Apostolos had laughed along with the others, he respected Thor. She could hear it in his voice. He wasn't as gruff with him as he was with the others, and she'd heard Frank grumbling about how only Thor was a sure thing for the next job.

"Thor is always on the callback list," Archie, another man on the crew, had said. "You know that."

And best of all, Thor believed her. It was in the way he examined what was left of the drill string, and the sincerity in his voice last night. In the morning, she would go to him and ask him to plead her case with Apostolos. As much as she hated to ask anyone for help, she couldn't figure out an alternative. She kept picturing Zach, and how she'd promised him karate lessons this year. His friends kept busy running from activity to activity. Flora knew her son longed to join them, but she'd never had the money. The contract with the oil company had changed that. It had the potential to change a lot of things if it lasted long enough. But if she had to work in a lab again, she'd be lucky if she could afford to buy her son a new jacket.

Her decision made, Flora rolled onto her stomach, pressing her cheek into the damp pillow. She still didn't sleep, but the pressure on her chest subsided until it no longer felt like a heart attack. Closing her eyes, she waited for daylight.

* * *

She'd been lurking outside the men's quarters for two hours before the first man stumbled out of his bunk. As soon as Flora heard him fumbling with the door, she was on her feet, ignoring the sharp crack from both her knees. Her ass was numb from sitting on the cold floor.

But it wasn't Thor. It was another man whose name she couldn't remember. He jumped when he saw her, narrowly missing hitting his head on the doorframe.

"Jesus Christ—you scared me to death. What the hell are you doing out here?"

She was about to apologize, and then remembered the conversation of the previous night. Maybe this man hadn't been a part of it, but he hadn't put a stop to it, either.

Flora straightened to her full height, lifting her chin. "I need to speak to Thor."

"Well, you'll be waiting awhile. He's always the last one to haul his sorry carcass out of bed." With a distasteful snuffling sound, he pushed past her, muttering something about having to piss.

Whatever his name was, he was right about Thor. Flora fidgeted while the other men slowly left the cabin and went about their business. Most didn't bother to acknowledge her, but they had plenty to say once they were safely past. How did women ever get pegged as the gossips? From what Flora had witnessed, guys were way worse.

She'd almost given up when Thor finally appeared, a faint shadow of stubble on his chin and crumbs of sleep in the corners of his eyes. She stepped forward to block his path.

"Good morning."

"Oh," he said, his eyes widening. "Sorry, I almost didn't see you. I'm a zombie before I have my coffee. How'd you sleep?"

How long had it been since a man—anyone, actually—had asked her that question? Five years, six? She'd lost count.

"Not well." Taking a deep breath, she decided to come out with it. "To tell the truth, I'm afraid of losing this job, Thor."

He lowered his gaze and rubbed his whiskery chin.

"I heard what the guys were saying last night. I heard what *Apostolos* said."

"I'm sorry, Flora. I tried to reason with them, but they weren't having any of it."

She sighed. "I know; I heard. Thank you for trying. It's more than anyone else did."

"I know some of that stuff must have been hard to hear, but the guys were only having a bit of a laugh. As you must have noticed, there isn't a lot for entertainment around here."

"And the sole woman on board makes for a hell of a joke."

"It's not like that. It wasn't you they were laughing at. It was your…" Thor groped for the right word. "*Theory.*"

Flora folded her arms across her chest. She'd promised herself she'd stay calm, but she could feel her temper rising. "You saw those teeth marks. What do you think it was?"

He glanced behind her, even though they were alone in the narrow hallway. Thor leaned closer, close enough that she could smell his stale breath. "To be honest, I think the guys are a little freaked out. No one can explain what happened to the drill, and no one wants to think about it much. You're a convenient scapegoat."

"I have a son, Thor. I'm raising him on my own. I really need this job."

"I'm sorry," he said, unable to meet her eyes. Instead he studied his sneakers, which were tied with sloppy bows. "But you'll find another ship. *The Cormorant* isn't the only game in town."

Flora's mind reeled. *Is he really that obtuse, or is he trying to get rid of me?* "Are you serious? After Apostolos is finished, my name will be mud. You heard him last night. He won't stop until no one will hire me."

He shifted his weight from foot to foot as if he had to use the head, which he probably did, considering he'd just woken up. "Apostolos can be vengeful if he's double-crossed, sure, but I don't think he'd do that to you. He thinks you're incompetent, not someone worth blacklisting."

"Well, that makes me feel a lot better. I'm sure there are tons of people who would go out of their way to hire an incompetent oceanographer. And you know what the worst of it is? I'm not incompetent. I'm actually really good at my job. They just refuse to hear what I have to say."

"What do you want from me, Flora? I tried to talk to them last night. You heard it yourself—they won't listen to me."

She had to restrain herself from grabbing the front of his grimy shirt. "I want you to talk to Apostolos. Convince him to give me another chance. If anyone can do it, it's you."

He raised an eyebrow. "I think you have an exaggerated view of my importance. Why would Apostolos listen to anything I have to say? He's the captain. I'm just a grunt. People like him don't listen to people like me."

He's not dumb, then. Only obtuse.

"He listens to you all the time, Thor. Sometimes I think you're the only one he does listen to. Why do you think I came to you? I need your help."

Thor frowned and ran a hand through his tousled hair. Like most of the men, he could have used a barber, but his need was more desperate than the others. His hair was so long in front he was beginning to resemble a sheepdog.

After a moment, during which Flora's stomach tied itself into knots, he shook his head. "That won't work."

"How do you know if you don't try?" Her fists clenched, her nails digging painfully into the skin.

"Apostolos isn't the type to change his mind once he's set on something, especially if I tell him he should. If anything, that will make him more stubborn."

She'd seen enough of the captain's behavior to know Thor was right. If one of the other men had told her the same, she would have accused them of making excuses, but his words had the ring of truth. "So there's no hope."

Flora was already considering how she'd break the news to Zach. Maybe she could teach him karate herself. She'd never taken a single class, but they had tutorials for everything on YouTube these days. It wouldn't be the same, but once she explained the situation to her son, she knew he'd understand. He'd shrug his little shoulders and say, "That's okay, Mom. Don't worry about it." Sometimes it broke her heart how accustomed he was to receiving bad news. It didn't even faze him anymore.

Why did I go ahead and open my fat mouth? Why did I make that stupid promise? I should have waited until the check was in the bank—or at least in the mail.

Thor's next words were enough to snap her out of her funk. "I wouldn't say that. Talking won't work, but you know what they say—a picture is worth a thousand words."

"You're not suggesting…"

"There's no permanent obstruction. You believe a large creature destroyed the drill. Correct?"

"Correct, but—"

"So what we need is evidence. We'll *show* Apostolos you were right. He won't be able to argue with that."

"Assuming there is such a creature, how do we know it will still be there? That's like expecting a shark or a fish to stay in one place and never move. It doesn't happen." But even as she said the words, Flora wasn't so sure. She knew there was something down there, and she suspected it was still close. She wasn't sure how she knew, and she wouldn't have confessed this to a living soul, but…she could feel it *waiting.* "And say it *is* there. How am I going to get a photograph? You're talking about an area that's thousands of feet under the surface. We don't have the equipment to get a diver down there."

"But we don't have to go that far. The drill was attacked near the surface. All we have to do is find something we can use as bait. If the creature is down there, it might attack again. And this time, we'll be ready."

In spite of the hot closeness of the hold, she shivered. "You're not suggesting putting a man down there. We have no idea what this creature is, or how it will react. No one would agree to do something that suicidal."

Thor grinned. "Ah, but if they don't believe there's anything down there, it's not suicidal, is it?"

CHAPTER SIX

Thor could see the terror in the big man's eyes. It was clear his bravado was nothing but an act—and not a very convincing one.

"Absolutely not. Nothin' doing. There's no way you're getting me in the water with that...that *thing*."

To be fair, they'd chosen the strongest man among them. Flora was reluctant to put any of the crew in danger, but if anyone could handle the risk, it was George.

No one had expected such a violent reaction. George's eyes rolled until they were showing almost all white, like a nervous horse.

Ah-ha! Thor attempted to hide a smirk but failed miserably. "So you *do* think there's something down there."

"Nah," George said, pointing at Flora, "I think she's crazy. But I've seen horror movies. I know how this goes. You crackers always make the black man go first. I'm not an idiot. I'm not going to fix any generator, I'm not going to investigate the scary noise, and I'm *definitely* not going in the water."

He folded his arms, making his biceps pop more than usual. He glowered at them while sweat pooled under Thor's collar.

"We asked you because you're the strongest, George—not because you're expendable. You're also one of the smartest," Flora said.

The huge man snorted at that, rolling his eyes. George resembled Michael Clarke Duncan in *The Green Mile*, except he looked nowhere near as friendly. "Damn right I'm smart. Too smart to get in that water. Find yourselves another sucker."

He shoved past them, clipping Flora with a shoulder as he passed. She lost her balance and crashed against the side of the ship. If George noticed, they couldn't tell. The air was lighter once he left.

Thor shrugged, giving Flora a sheepish grin. "Well, there goes that plan. Guess we have to find someone a little less superstitious."

"This is too much to ask of anyone. It's too dangerous. We don't know what we're dealing with down there, if anything. I'm not comfortable asking anyone to risk his life." Flora rubbed at her forehead as if she were trying to scrub the skin off. She probably had another headache. She was sick an awful lot—not that he blamed her. Living at sea took a bit of getting used to. At least she wasn't puking her guts out like some of the new guys did.

"What are our choices? Either we convince Apostolos you're telling the truth, or you'll lose your job as soon as we return to port."

She straightened, and her face took on that determined expression again—the same expression that had convinced a lot of the guys she was a stone-cold bitch. But Thor suspected Flora was only tough when she had to be. "I'll do it."

"No." He shook his head, echoing George. "Absolutely not."

"It *has* to be me. It's the only thing that makes sense. It's my theory and my job that's on the line. I'm a great swimmer and a certified diver. And I have the most experience with marine animals."

"Whatever is down there shattered a steel drill into pieces. I don't think you're going to get the chance to Dr. Doolittle it."

"No one is going to stick out his neck for me, Thor. You saw George's reaction. They don't believe me, but they don't want to risk it, either. And I don't blame them."

Thor was too exhausted to argue. He sank down on the deck, sighing. "For a woman with so many degrees, you're pretty dense. Let's say you go down there and that thing appears. Just for fun, let's say you survive. Why should Apostolos believe you? Once again, it's your word against ours. Of course you would say the creature exists. Why wouldn't you? It's your theory."

Flora frowned. "You're right. No one would believe me."

"I would, but that's the reason it can't be me, either. We have to find someone else. And they'll need to take a camera."

* * *

They found Liam—Liam of the shy smile and wire-rimmed glasses. Thor didn't want to ask him. He was one of the only guys on the ship Thor could stand. Unlike the others, Liam didn't consider *Playboy* fine literature, and he believed that clipping one's toenails and cleaning one's nose were best done in private.

Thor knew *something* was down there. The teeth marks were proof. But he suspected it was a shark, or maybe a giant squid—something with a logical explanation that would have moved on by now. And if not, he was confident he could get Liam on deck fast if he had to.

"You can't be serious," Liam said when they asked him, but his smile soon vanished when he saw their expressions.

"*Please*, Liam. Flora needs this job. She has a kid to feed, and she's on her own. If we don't get someone to corroborate her theory, Apostolos is going to can her."

Liam's brown eyes softened as he considered Flora, and Thor knew they'd found the right guy. He may not have had the strength of George, but he was younger and faster. George was so big he'd probably have sunk like a stone. "I was raised by a single mother," he said.

"There you go." Thor clapped him on the shoulder. "You'll help us, then?"

He gave them a wary look that Thor instantly understood. Men got bored living in close quarters like this. The practical jokes could get vile in a hurry. Thor glanced at Flora, who appeared to read his mind.

"I really appreciate your bravery, but I understand if you don't feel comfortable with it. We'll do everything we can to keep you safe, and if you get into trouble, all you have to do is tug on the line," she said. "We'll pull you up. Still, you should know there are no guarantees. We have no idea what we're dealing with."

"Wait—you don't actually think there's a sea monster down there?" Liam looked from Flora to Thor, waiting for the punch line. "You can't be serious. I thought it was a prank."

"You saw those teeth marks," Thor said. "What do you think made them, a fish?"

"We're not saying there's a sea monster. I'm sure there's a logical explanation for what happened to the drill string," Flora added. "But whatever made those marks is extremely strong, extremely large, and highly aggressive. If you decide to do this, you should know what you're risking."

Liam fell silent for a moment, considering. Thor wanted nothing more than to get the show on the road—soon the ship would be moving again, and then it would be too late. But Flora had told him not to press. If anyone agreed to help, it had to be of his own free will.

After what seemed like hours, Liam shrugged. "Sure. Why not?"

"Great, let's get you suited." Before Thor could rush him below deck, Flora stopped them. Her eyes were damp, and the hand she put on Liam's shoulder trembled slightly.

"Are you sure? We'll do everything we can, but we can't guarantee your safety."

Thor held his breath, positive she'd just fucked everything up. Liam didn't strike him as the most courageous guy in the world.

But Liam only grinned. "Why not? Until we get under way again, there's nothing else to do.

"Besides, everyone knows there's no such thing as sea monsters."

CHAPTER SEVEN

Something was wrong.

The dread that hovered over Flora had grown stronger once Liam agreed to Thor's plan. She had to bite her lip to keep from talking the young man out of it. She'd already said too much, which had earned her an elbow in the ribs.

But she couldn't help it. That heavy feeling of foreboding increased until she wanted to run to her cabin and lock herself in. When Liam joined them on deck, dressed in scuba gear, it was all she could do not to block his way, screaming doomsday warnings.

While Liam was fiddling with the oxygen tank, she grabbed Thor's arm. "We can't let him go down there."

Thor stared at her like she was insane. "What are you talking about? Of course we can. It's your one chance."

Flora tried to stay calm, but her head was pounding so much she could barely think. "I don't care about the job. Forget it. Nothing's worth someone's life."

"Liam's life isn't at risk, any more than it ever was. You know the plan—if he gets in trouble, he just—"

"Pulls the line, I know. But what if he doesn't have time? What if we're not fast enough?"

A wave of nausea rippled through her stomach, signaling an oncoming anxiety attack. *Oh God, not here. Not now.* Her forehead broke out in a sweat, and she doubled over, clutching her abdomen.

"Flora?"

Liam stood over her, his brow furrowed with concern. He hesitated, then put a hand on her shoulder. "Are you okay?"

"I—I haven't been feeling well." It was close enough to the truth. There was no need to reveal the cause of her illness.

"I heard you guys talking, and I wanted to tell you I'll be fine. I'm not worried. Did you know I was born in the Maldives? I was practically raised in the ocean."

She managed a smile. "With a name like Liam?"

"My mom is Irish." He shrugged.

"No one is doubting your diving skills. It's just that...you saw what happened to the drill. We don't know what this creature is, or even if it's still down there. We can't predict its behavior. It wouldn't be safe."

"Don't worry. I'm not afraid of fictional creatures," he said with the conviction of the young. "If it doesn't exist, it can't hurt me."

"And how do you explain what happened to the drill string?" Flora asked, fighting to keep her breathing slow and even. Her heart felt like it would explode from her chest at any moment. "Those teeth marks certainly aren't a figment of my imagination."

"The human mind is highly susceptible. Some people see the Virgin Mary in a piece of toast. You're an oceanographer, so you're conditioned to see a Holy Grail of another sort—proof that a mythical creature actually exists."

"I didn't *see* anything. That's the problem. We have no idea what we're dealing with. Why isn't anyone *listening* to me?" She needed to stop talking in order to catch her breath. Using both hands, she pressed hard on her diaphragm, willing the panic that was welling inside her to stay where it belonged. Thor stepped in between them, shooting her a worried glance.

"Flora is a scientist. She's no more prone to flights of fancy than you or I, and if she says those are teeth marks, it's like one of us saying the Bernoulli Equation exists. I'd take her word for it."

Liam grinned. "So you believe in the monster too? I didn't think you were the type, Thor."

The temper that had gotten her into so much trouble in her youth bubbled to the surface. She elbowed Thor aside and closed the distance between her and Liam until their noses were nearly touching. She was gratified when Liam retreated a step.

"Something is *wrong* here—can't you feel it? Something bad is going to happen if you get in that water."

For a moment, she thought they were feeling it too. That their hackles were rising, the skin on their arms and necks pimpling into goose bumps. Then Liam laughed, raising an eyebrow at Thor.

"Yep, that's pretty scientific, all right. She's got a bad feeling. Can't argue with that."

Her temper got the best of her then, and although she knew she'd probably regret it for the rest of her life, the heat of her anger made her *want* to show him. Let him laugh when he came face to face with whatever lurked beneath the surface.

Praying she'd be able to forgive herself, she let him go.

* * *

"You promise not to let go of the line?"

Liam nodded, tightening his grip on the towline. It was impossible to make out his expression under the mask, but without his glasses, his eyes were larger than usual. Was he finally showing some sense? Was he frightened? That flicker of fear, that widening of the eyes, was all she got before Liam saluted them and strode to the side of the ship.

"Don't worry. If it was an animal that did this, it's probably long gone," Thor said, grunting with the effort as he guided his colleague over the side of the boat to the ladder that would take him to the surface. "Liam's sharp. If he sees anything that worries him, he only has to tug on the line and I'll have him out in two shakes."

"And how's he going to see a bloody thing? We blinded him." Her voice cracked on the last word, and she relaxed her grip on Liam's wire-rimmed spectacles. He'd handed them to her before putting on the diving mask. The rage that had temporarily rendered her uncaring had vanished. Instead, she wondered what she would tell Liam's mother.

"He's far-sighted, Flora. Unless the creature is nose to nose with him, he'll see it in plenty of time."

She clutched the side of the boat, inhaling the briny air. There was nothing to do but wait. Wait, and hope that Thor was right.

"What in the name of Christ are you two doing?"

Thor jumped nearly as high as Flora. Thank God he managed to keep a hold on the towline—what she'd begun to think of as Liam's lifeline.

"Liam went for a dive, sir."

Flora was astounded at the speed with which Thor threw his friend under the bus. It was second nature to these jerks.

"A dive?" Apostolos turned a new and interesting shade of purple as he stormed across the deck toward them. It took everything she had not to cringe at the large man's approach. "Why in the hell would he do something so asinine? Has he been taking retard lessons from you, Anderssen?"

"Not that I'm aware of, sir."

"Then it was probably you that talked him into it, wasn't it?" Apostolos spat the words at her, his face so close she could smell the garlic on his breath. "Are you trying to get everyone on this bloody barge fired so they can join you in the unemployment line?"

"Not that you'll listen to me, but I tried to talk him out of it. I don't think it's safe."

She was relieved when he pushed past her to lean over the edge of the ship, his thick brows furrowing. "Damn right it's not safe. We're about to push off to get new materials. If I hadn't gotten the mind to check on you idiots, Lashay would have been left behind. If our props didn't get him, the sharks would have."

"He was determined to get a glimpse of the creature, sir."

"Would you pull the wax outta your ears, Anderssen? There isn't any creature out there, at least nothing we don't already know about. I'm not sure what you've got between you, but you need to get it through your thick skull that she's no more a scientist than she is a sailor."

Thor cleared his throat. "I don't believe that, sir."

"Are you contradicting me? On my own ship? You'd like to join your girlfriend in the welfare office, is that what you're telling me?"

"Don't bother, Thor. It's not worth it," Flora said. She had the measure of the captain now, even more than before, and there was nothing Thor could say or do that would change his mind.

"Why are you standing there, flapping your gums at me?" Apostolos bellowed, growing even darker in the face. "Bring him up."

She'd never expected to agree with Apostolos about anything, but it didn't matter why Liam was pulled to the surface, as long as he was safe.

It would have been a good day for diving, had there been anything to see. The ocean was calm for a change. Unusually calm, come to think of it. Its surface was a shimmering aquamarine, as flat and placid as a lake.

The only thing that disturbed the surface was a series of ripples that expanded and collapsed into one another, following each other like train cars on a rail. Flora's fingers tightened on the rough wood of the railing as she leaned over the side for a better look. The ripples were moving faster now, and coming closer. They were headed right for Liam. That sense that something was wrong increased until Flora thought she would scream. Before Apostolos could say anything else, she seized his arm and pointed, not even noticing when he shook her off hard enough to make her wrist crack.

"Thor, get him out of there. Hurry—something's coming." Her heart fluttered like a bird desperate to escape its cage. A wave of heat rushed over her, and her legs trembled, threatening to deposit her on the deck.

And then the towline went nuts.

Frustrated by Thor's feeble attempts to haul Liam to safety, Apostolos shoved him out of the way. Swearing, he pulled the line in hand over fist, his thick arms bulging with the effort.

Tears slid down Flora's cheeks, but she didn't notice. Even though she hadn't been to church since she was a child, she began to pray. She figured it couldn't hurt, and reciting the familiar words kept her from running around the deck shrieking.

"There he is," Apostolos yelled, and Flora felt overwhelming gratitude as she saw Liam surface. He appeared to be just the same as when they'd lowered the line, except that he was trying to clamber up the tow rope as if a demon were after him. The line jerked and swayed under his efforts, and Apostolos cursed him and his mother and any future children he might have. "Stay still, you dumb bastard, or I'll put you in there myself."

For an agonizing moment, Flora watched as Liam clung to the rope, his mouth working around his regulator. He was trying to tell them something.

"Don't just stand there—*do* something. Get him out of there," she screamed. As the strange ripples moved ever closer to the boat, the ship itself began to buck and sway, as if traveling over gigantic waves, though the sea was still calm as glass. The deck creaked ominously, and Flora could feel the wood shudder beneath her feet.

Jolted into action, Thor rushed to help Apostolos. With both men pulling the rope, the process went much faster. Soon Liam was crouching, wet and shaking, on the deck. The ripples glided past where he had been only moments before.

Everyone froze as the ship rocked violently from side to side.

And then the ocean was calm once more.

Liam ripped out his respirator, gasping and choking. Flora ran to get him some fresh water and a towel, her pulse pounding in her ears. The threat of her panic attack had receded, as it did whenever a genuine crisis was at hand.

By the time she returned, the men had helped Liam out of his wetsuit. He was unharmed, but his skin was the color of ashes and he shook uncontrollably. Flora tossed the towel to Thor, who wrapped it around the trembling man. When Liam spotted Flora, he started to babble, his eyes wide and scared in his pale face.

"I saw it. It was massive. It was gigantic...truly monstrous." His words were cut off by a violent fit of coughing. Once his choking had subsided, Flora pressed the glass of water into his shaking hands. He had to use both of them to guide the glass to his mouth.

"Let's get him below deck. This man has suffered a shock. He needs to rest," Apostolos ordered. "Enough standing around gawking. Duchovney, you take Lashay to his quarters. Anderssen, I need your help at the controls. I want to get out of this place."

Thor hesitated, but Flora waved him on. She could handle the young engineer, who didn't weigh much more than she did. Besides, maybe Liam would talk about what he'd seen if another guy wasn't around. She hooked Liam's arm around her shoulders and guided him toward the stairs.

Apostolos didn't spare them a glance, but he was in an uncommon hurry to get things underway. While he was always all business, he usually had the relaxed lassitude of a man whose check was already in the bank. Not today.

As the captain passed them, Flora was stunned to see a foreign expression on the big Greek's face.

Apostolos was afraid.

CHAPTER EIGHT

They were lucky it was me.

If it had been my wife, they wouldn't have been talking and laughing and sharing stories, I can tell you that. Their little ship would have been smashed to smithereens, and all that would have remained of their bodies would have been the odd tooth or bit of bone.

My wife didn't like to play.

On the other hand, I was always up for entertainment. Life got tedious without it, enough that I often envied the smaller creatures who needed to have things like survival instincts. Our kind doesn't have survival instincts. We just are.

Though our species had long communicated telepathically, I had never experienced that link with any other creature, and yet I had access to the geologist's thoughts. Sometimes I could even view what was happening on the ship through her eyes. This unexpected mind meld was as disturbing as it was fascinating. *Why this human? And why now?* I had to find out.

Humans, while a nuisance, were definitely entertaining.

Their misguided confidence was amusing. Thinking they could pull that scrawny specimen away before I got to him—*ha*. If I'd bothered to stretch out my neck, I could have bitten him in half before those idiots knew what happened. It was tempting. The commotion that would have occurred when they hauled that broken, bloody mess on board would have been priceless. Nothing was music to our ears like the sound of humans leaving our waters.

But something stopped me. He was so puny, so helpless, thrashing around on that rope. I could have eaten the entire ship and not suffered so much as a stomachache. But if I let him live, perhaps he would warn his fellow idiots. I'm sure they'd take their nasty drills somewhere else, but at least they'd be someone else's problem, threatening someone else's home.

I hadn't revealed myself to a human for at least three centuries, and I admit I was curious about their reaction. I suspected modern humans thought themselves more sophisticated than their ancestors. It was obvious they were desensitized to violence, desensitized to the supernatural, desensitized to even their own suffering. Would they be desensitized to me?

On the first pass, I glided close enough that the human could feel my wake but would not be able to see me. It worked. The acrid stench of his fear was so strong I could almost taste it. His confidence on the ship had been nothing but bravado. Once he was in the water, he was in my territory, and he knew it.

There was one thing I'd always envied about the humans, although I'd never admit it to my wife. They had tremendous survival instincts. They always knew when some danger was lurking, or when they were about to die. What I'd never been able to figure out is why they never paid attention to them.

From several leagues away, I could see the man's hands tighten on the rope. He wasn't giving a signal—not yet—but he wanted to, that much was obvious. He knew something wasn't right. His tiny legs flailed as he panicked, pushing small fish and other curious creatures aside. The man didn't even acknowledge them. He was waiting for me.

Another pass, and this time I came closer. *Too* close. I'm afraid I might have damaged their little boat. Hopefully not enough to stop them from leaving. Then the wife would surely get involved.

The man had a little device held close to his face, and I immediately knew what it was. Uisge had warned us about these foul machines often enough. It would preserve my image and capture it for the people on land to see. I could be famous like our poor cousin. For a moment, I was tempted to bare my teeth at the puny thing so he could take his precious picture, but common sense prevailed. I merely flicked my tail at him, but that was enough.

To see him scramble up that rope with his gear and those ridiculous fins on his feet! I hadn't laughed so hard in years. I was still angry about the damage that had been done to my home, but I decided to let them live, in return for the entertainment. At least humans were more amusing than fish.

By the time I returned home, the wife was in a lather.

"Where have you been, Nøkken? I see you haven't brought us any food."

The sneer on her face dissolved my good mood. At her side, my son whined with hunger. I'd never understood why my wife insisted that I do most of the hunting. She was much more skilled at it than I.

"Our dinner has found a new hiding place. Not much out and about today, but I'll try again in a few." In truth, I'd found plenty. A full school of tarpon and several tiger sharks had me stuffed. I cursed myself for not thinking to bring any home.

Her eyes narrowed. "You lie, Nøkken." Her tail poked me sharply in the underbelly, drawing blood. My son drifted after the tiny fish that gathered to feast on my essence, snapping his teeth with relish. I'd hoped he'd take after me rather than his mother, but it appeared I was losing that particular battle. As I'd done hundreds of times since his birth, I resolved to spend more time at home, even though I knew I wouldn't. Truth be told, I didn't much like our son. He was a temperamental sort, whose moods ranged from nasty to demanding. More than once I'd threatened to send him to live with his aunt. He mostly ignored me.

"Your belly protrudes. You have stuffed yourself again." She poked me once more for good measure. I winced, but tried not to snarl. Showing aggression would only make things worse.

"It was only a few sharks. Just a snack, nothing more. Shall I try again, sweetheart? I can bring something home for you and The Boy."

"You should have thought of that before. You are full of lies. Why is it that I feel more and more as if I shouldn't trust you?" As she circled me, I dared not meet her eyes. "What else have you been doing?"

"Nothing. Only surveying the territory, as always." My eyes downcast, I could feel her swirling around me. The mood in our lair was heavy, stifling. Clearly she'd been waiting awhile for me, growing angrier with every passing second. I should have brought the little ship home, given it to our son as a toy. That would have pleased her.

"The humans are gone?"

"What?" I was startled by the question, and it took every ounce of self-control not to react. Of course she would narrow in on the humans. She was still in a bad temper over what they'd done to our home, ignoring the fact that the worst of the damage had been caused by her.

"Tell me the truth, Nøkken, or I will go to the surface myself. Are the humans gone, or are they not?"

I thought of that tiny helpless ship and the even tinier men aboard. Though I'd been able to calm her the first time, my wife would destroy them now without thinking twice. Centuries ago I would have done the same, but something gave me pause. Why I felt sympathy toward these particular humans was a curious thing, but it was something I was determined to discover for myself. So few things required deeper thought these days.

"They are gone." I risked looking my wife in the eye as I said it, and thankfully my words appeared to satisfy her.

"Too bad. They would have made an adequate amuse-bouche for our son." She moved past me and flicked her tail at the child, beckoning. "Come, Boy. Let's go get you some food, since your father hasn't seen fit to share his bounty with us."

They barely made a wake as they left. Both Draugen and her boy were graceful swimmers.

I breathed a sigh of relief. Settling down for a nap, I thought once more of the humans and their ship. They'd better be gone by tomorrow.

Their lives depended on it.

CHAPTER NINE

"You have to calm down. You've been through a terrible shock. Try to get some rest."

Liam seized Flora's wrist with surprising strength. "Don't leave. Stay with me. I can't…I can't be alone right now."

"All right, I'll stay for a bit. But you have to calm down, or you'll get us both in trouble. And you have to let me go."

The engineer released her immediately. She shook her hand to get the blood flowing again. He may have been scrawny, but he wasn't nearly as weak as he appeared.

"I saw it, Flora. I really saw it." His eyes were huge, and she feared he was going to panic again. She patted his hand in an attempt to comfort him, and wished for Thor, but Thor was helping Apostolos. The sad truth was, she was the only person on the boat who was seen as expendable. Her help was never needed.

"You need to rest. Please lie down."

Every time his head touched the pillow, he bolted upright again, gasping in terror. And even though she understood what a panic attack felt like better than anyone aboard, she didn't know how to help him. She didn't know Liam. Before that day, they'd barely spoken two words to each other. How was she to comfort him?

"If I lie down, you'll leave." He reached for her arm again, but this time, she was fast enough to move out of range. He was going to bruise her if she wasn't careful.

"I won't; I promise. I'll stay with you until the guys return."

"I don't want to talk to the guys. They won't believe me. They'll just make my life miserable, like—" An anguished expression came over his face. "Like they did to you. I'm so sorry. And I was just as bad. I'm such an idiot."

"It's okay." Flora glanced at the doorway, hoping against hope that Thor would be finished his duties soon and come relieve her. But outside the room it was dark and quiet. The creaking of the ship unnerved her. Why weren't they moving? She wasn't sure how long she'd been with Liam, but it felt like hours. "Try not to think about it."

She felt awkward sitting on the edge of his bunk, and there wasn't enough room.

"I should have listened to you. I didn't believe—no, that's not right. I didn't *want* to believe you were telling the truth. But I saw it, Flora."

All right, Liam. Obviously you're not going to rest until you tell your story, so let's get it over with. "What did you see?"

To her horror, the young man started to cry, tears rolling down his cheeks. "The sea monster," he said in a harsh whisper. "I saw the sea monster."

She stifled her impulse to remind him there was no such thing as sea monsters. Liam obviously believed he'd seen one, and in any case, it was common for people to refer to unidentified creatures as monsters. There was no doubt in her mind that whatever Liam had seen was uncategorized. The state of the drill string had told her that much. "What did it look like?"

"I didn't see much of it. Thankfully, it didn't get close enough," he admitted. "But it was huge—gigantic. Bigger than a whale. Bigger than my apartment complex. And bigger than this ship. *A lot* bigger."

Flora bit her lower lip, a habit left over from when she was a girl whose words always got her into trouble. It was impossible for the creature to be that big. For one thing, someone would have seen it long before now, and for another, what did it eat? What could possibly sustain something that size?

Liam slumped against his pillow, defeated. "You don't believe me, do you?"

"It's not that. It's only—" She struggled to find the right words, to be diplomatic. Unfortunately, diplomacy was not something she excelled at. *Fuck. Where was Thor?* "I'm sure the water distorted its size. It isn't possible for the creature to be that large."

"I'm an engineer, remember? I know the size of things, and I'm telling you this wasn't an optical illusion. The thing was *huge*. It would make a blue whale look like a tadpole."

"What else did you see?" Changing the subject was probably the best way to handle the disagreement without it turning into an argument. But it would be a cold day in hell before she'd believe a creature that enormous could stay hidden for long.

"It had a long neck. And a long tail. It swiped me with it when it turned around, and my leg's been hurting ever since. I'm scared to look at it."

Flora felt the air leave her lungs as the pressure returned to her chest full force. She'd known Liam was in shock and half hysterical, but he'd never said anything about being hurt. The ship had no doctor, of course. Since she was a woman, the crew expected her to be on top of things like bandages and antiseptic spray. And because they were men, they never expected to need a doctor in the first place.

"Can I see?"

When he nodded, she moved closer, looking at the door again before lifting the blanket. Praying the guys wouldn't choose that moment to return, she helped the young man struggle out of the damp wetsuit. Before the suit was at his hips, she saw the blood.

"It's bad, isn't it?" He studied her face while his own grew paler. "It's really bad, right? I knew it—I should have listened to you. Then none of this would have happened."

Privately, she agreed with him, but this wasn't the time to rub it in. "Sshhh…I won't know anything until I get a closer look at it." Liam propped himself on his elbows, staring down at his leg, but she gently pushed him away. "Try to relax."

His leg was so swollen she wouldn't be able to pull the suit off without injuring him further. It had acted like a compression bandage, but now that they'd relieved some of the pressure, an astonishing amount of blood was flowing over his stomach. Luckily she had brought the ship's meager first-aid kit with her, just in case. "I'm going to need to cut the suit off in order to bandage your leg. Is that all right?"

To her relief, he agreed, and for the first time, she noticed how weak he was. He had already lost a lot of blood. She had to keep him from losing any more. Swallowing hard against any queasiness, she took out her Swiss Army knife and began to saw through the legs of the wetsuit. The sound of the neoprene tearing filled the room and ended any need for conversation. He kept his eyes focused on the bunk above him, but Flora noticed he gripped the blanket with both hands.

"Am I hurting you?"

"No. Just…scared."

His leg was swelling before her eyes, looking less and less like a limb and more like an overstuffed sausage. It was likely the pressure from the suit, which was now several sizes too small, that caused him pain. Frustrated with the lack of progress, Flora took a deep breath and grasped both sides of the cut she'd made. Pulling hard, she split the suit's leg to the crotch, not missing Liam's wince.

It took all the self-control she had not to gasp. Liam's leg was an angry purple where the circulation had been cut off, but that wasn't the worst. Three gashes exposed the meat of his leg, revealing flesh that looked like raw steak. A wave of heat and nausea swept over her, and she closed her eyes, focusing on slow and steady breathing. *I cannot faint. I must not faint.*

"It's serious, isn't it?"

At the sound of Liam's voice, she opened her eyes. In his terror, he had regressed to a boy about Zach's age, and her motherly instincts kicked in. She squeezed his hand, but before she could reassure him, he cut her off.

"Don't lie to me. I can tell how bad it is by the look on your face. I'm going to die, aren't I?"

"Of course you're not going to die." Unless he got gangrene or some other blood infection, but she wouldn't dwell on that. The edges of the wounds were red and oozing, and she prayed the creature that made them hadn't been venomous. "But I can't bandage these cuts. They'll have to be sewn."

"Go ahead. I can take it." She could see the muscles in his jaw clench as he gritted his teeth. Flora felt lightheaded as her earlier panic attack threatened to return.

"What do you mean, 'go ahead'?"

"Stitch me. I'll try my best not to scream."

"I can't do that—I can't sew. One of the guys will have to do it."

Liam stared at her like she'd suggested amputation. "Are you crazy? I'm not letting those lumbering oafs near me with a needle. You have to do it, Flora."

She thought of the one time she'd attempted to save some money by sewing a button on Zach's coat herself. She'd sewn the coat to her jeans, and the button had still fallen off.

"I've spent all my time in labs, Liam. I'm not exactly domestically gifted. Let me staunch the bleeding, and I'll see what I can do." Part of her was drifting outside herself, marveling at this Oscar-worthy performance. She actually sounded calm.

The bandages in the first-aid kit were not going to cut it. Flora ran to her cabin for one of her sheets, which she assumed were much cleaner than anything in the men's cabins. Tearing the sheet into strips, she splashed rubbing alcohol on them, rinsed Liam's leg with water, and tied the makeshift bandages around the wounds. She'd suspected Liam would fight with her about going upstairs for help, but she needn't have worried. He'd fallen unconscious by the time she finished, either from the pain or the shock.

* * *

As it turned out, Frank was the one who sewed Liam's leg, having done some time as a medic in the navy. "Idiotic kid," he muttered as Liam moaned in his sleep. "Could have fucking died. Why didn't he tell anyone he was hurt?"

"I think he was scared." Flora was as far away as she could get while still being able to hear what was happening. She leaned on the doorframe and rubbed her queasy stomach. The three Pepto-Bismols Thor had given her hadn't helped.

"Dying is a whole lot scarier than getting stitches," Frank said. "There. Done. Somebody hand me some scissors so I don't have to cut this damn thread with my teeth."

There was something eerily Frankenstein's monster-like about Liam's leg, which was now zigzagged by ugly black stitches, but Flora had to admit Frank had done a masterful job. He was as neat as the cosmetic surgeon who'd sewn her son's forehead after Zach took a tumble from his treehouse. If Liam was lucky, he might not even have much of a scar.

When Frank brushed past her, Flora hesitated before reaching out to touch the man's arm. He had always unnerved her the most, after Apostolos. She had never seen him smile, and he resembled a criminal more than a sailor. But perhaps she had misjudged him. Although he'd tried his best to seem irritated, he'd shown more tenderness with Liam than she could have hoped. "Thank you."

He shrugged. "Someone had to do it. I think I've earned myself a few beers, that's what I think."

"Will he be all right?"

Frank glanced over at Liam, who was still sleeping. The younger man was still unnaturally pale, but at least a little color had begun to seep into his cheeks. "Yep; no thanks to him, though. As soon as he's upright again, he's going to have to go a few rounds with me."

The sailor left, and Thor moved to leave as well. "Join us for a drink? There isn't anything else you can do for him right now."

She shook her head. "Someone should be here when he wakes. You didn't see him earlier. He was so panicked and scared. I don't think he'd handle it well if he's left alone tonight."

"Can I bring you something, then?"

"Not for me, but Liam could probably use some water."

"You got it. Waters all around."

He patted her shoulder as he walked by, but she called him before he could reach the stairs.

"I overheard you guys talking and you seemed pretty upset. Was it about Liam, or something else?"

Thor frowned. "It wasn't Liam. We didn't even know he was hurt until you told us. It's a good thing you stayed with him. Frank's right. He would have died if you hadn't found out about that cut."

The notion was enough to make her shiver. "If it wasn't Liam, then what?"

"Something's wrong with the engine. Whatever hit us after we pulled Liam out of the water must have thrown it out of whack. George and I couldn't get it going again."

Her nausea intensified. Flora clutched the doorframe for support. "What are you saying?"

"I'm saying we're stuck here until we can fix whatever's wrong or get someone to tow us in. But that's a long shot. Apostolos thinks no one is close enough to get to us in good time, so we're going to have to fix it ourselves."

Funny how things could change so drastically in a matter of hours. That morning, all she'd wanted was to convince Apostolos to let her stay, and now more than anything, she wished to be at home with her son. Maybe she could ask her parents to chip in for the karate lessons, because there was no way she was setting foot on a ship ever again.

She could hardly wait until the problem was solved and *The Cormorant* was gliding through the water, putting hundreds of miles between her and whatever death awaited them down below.

CHAPTER TEN

"So, you've all got your drinks? And you're sitting down, I can see that." Apostolos sounded grimmer than usual.

"Is it Lashay, boss? The kid's going to be okay, isn't he?" someone named Archie asked. Thor hadn't talked to him much, but he'd noticed the man stayed quiet whenever the other guys razzed him.

"The kid's going to be fine. Although we need some antibiotics. George, you still got some of the stuff you were taking for that ear infection?"

George grunted in assent.

"Make sure you give it to the woman tonight. Forget that bullshit about not sharing medication. If that kid gets an infection out here, he's royally fucked."

"I did my best, but he needs to get to a hospital as soon as possible. I didn't like the look of those cuts. He could be infected already. When are we underway?" Frank asked, his voice a low growl. A sheen of sweat glistened on his bald, bullet-shaped head.

Of all the people Thor would have expected to fight for Liam, Frank would have been his last choice. Thor was sure Liam would be similarly surprised when he woke up and discovered who had saved his life.

"That's why I wanted you sitting down. The ship is crippled. Until we're able to repair the engine, we're dead in the water," Apostolos said.

A chorus of protest rose from the table. Only George and Thor were silent.

"Whatever it is, we can't get at it topside. Someone is going to have to put on a wetsuit and take a peek at the hull, see if we can get at it that way."

Thor was glad he was sitting down. Apostolos hadn't shared that part of the plan before. The protests grew even louder.

"After what happened to the kid?" Frank asked. "It's suicide."

"We don't know what happened to him. My guess is he got himself all excited about this sea monster bullshit, saw a whale or something down there, and injured his leg climbing into the ship." Apostolos surveyed his crew, treating Frank and Thor to a withering glare. They were the only men who had been unfortunate enough to see Liam's leg—Frank in particular had seen it up close and personal—and there was no way in hell it got that injured from the kid climbing into the boat.

"I don't think anyone else should get in the water before we know it's safe. Have we picked up anything on sonar?" George asked. For some mysterious reason, he alone never seemed intimidated by Apostolos.

"Not a thing. It hasn't been working properly since the woman did her little survey." Apostolos smirked. "Appears she was right—there *is* something down there. Guess I'm going to have to find a different reason to fire her."

The Greek met Thor's eyes, silently challenging him to rush to Flora's defense, but the younger man kept his mouth shut. After what they'd seen that day, Thor didn't think Flora gave a rat's ass about keeping her job anymore.

"So we can't tell what's down there. Suicide, that's exactly what this is. With all due respect, *sir*, I don't think any of us is that big a fool." George crossed his huge arms and glowered at their boss.

"Don't you get it? It might be suicide to *stay*. Our problems started when we sent that string down. Suppose, just suppose, we're in this thing's territory. I don't plan to hang around here any longer than I have to."

There were a lot of uneasy looks being handed around the table. And then Thor felt that familiar urge, that irresistible impulse that his mom had predicted would get him killed one day.

"I'll go."

Everyone stared at him like he was crazy, but the truth was, he felt guilty for what had happened to Liam. He'd believed that some kind of creature was responsible for the destruction of the drill string, and he'd let Liam get in the water anyway.

"It's your life, kid. What's left of it, that is," George said, but Thor could see the relief written on his face. Even though the big man could have taken the rest of the crew on at once, he'd grown increasingly wary. Almost as if he thought they'd sneak up behind him and throw him overboard as bait the moment he wasn't on high alert.

"Absolutely not. It can't be Thor."

Frank sneered. "And why the hell not? Because he's the son you never had?"

Thor was shocked at the amount of vitriol in the man's voice. Guess people got more honest when they feared for their lives.

"No, asshole, because he can run this barge if something happens to me. You guys know this ship is a prototype—we're the only two on board who know how it works."

"I'm also your best mechanic now that Liam's out of commission," Thor said. "If you send one of the other guys down, they might not know what to look for."

He had Apostolos in a corner, and could see by his expression that the captain knew it. There were no cobwebs growing on the brains of Frank, George, and Archie, but they were oilmen and sailors. Maintaining the ship and other mechanical functions had always fallen to Liam and Thor. On the prototype, most of the operations were intended to be handled by robotics, greatly minimizing the costs of supporting a large crew. Unfortunately, this meant there wasn't a lot of available brainpower when things went wrong.

The men waited for the Greek's decision. The air in the room got so heavy Thor could barely breathe. This hadn't been the relaxing break he'd hoped for, and he wished he'd stayed in the cabin with Liam and Flora. At least he wouldn't have heard his colleagues accept his potential death with such ease. *Aw, who was I kidding? They were never my colleagues, not really.* They came from different worlds, different generations. All they had in common was the desire to make some decent money and have a bit of an adventure at the same time.

"How are you in the water, Anderssen?"

"I'm not a competitive diver like Liam, but I can hold my own. I've done enough dives to know I can stay submerged long enough to examine the ship."

"Tomorrow then. As soon as it's light, you'll meet me on deck. I want everyone else there as well, just in case there's more trouble."

Thor pushed away from the table. "I should relieve Flora now if I'm going to be awake that early. Who wants to take the third shift in a couple hours?"

The men glanced at each other as if Thor were speaking another language.

"What are you talking about, Anderssen?" The gruffness had returned to Apostolos's voice, making Thor wonder if he'd imagined the concern the captain had shown him only moments before.

"Liam's in a bad way, sir. If he wakes and finds himself alone, he might panic and do something stupid."

Frank snorted. "I think he's used up his quota of stupid for the day, kid. Wouldn't worry about that."

"He may need something, then. Some water. More painkillers. We can't leave him to suffer this out on his own. Flora thinks someone should stay with him, and I agree."

He ignored the mutters from Archie and Frank about how whipped he was. He couldn't help it if Flora was the only one who made any sense most of the time.

"The woman's with him now?" Apostolos asked. The way he never used her name bothered him. She was always "the woman" now. Thor couldn't remember whether it had always been that way.

"Yeah."

"Then let her stay with him. That's as good a job as any for her. God knows she won't be any use to us on the deck tomorrow."

"But she's an oceanographer with a degree in marine biology as well as a geologist. If anyone can figure out what this creature is and how to deal with it, it's her."

"I know how to deal with it. The last thing I need is that woman yapping in my ear about her theories. I've taken about all I can stand of that."

"We can't leave her there around the clock, sir. Someone has to relieve her eventually." Thor wondered if Flora had left Liam for a minute since the incident, even for a bathroom break or to get something to eat. He was pretty sure she hadn't.

Apostolos shrugged. "Let her stay there. If she decides there's something else she'd rather do, she can come see me."

He laughed then, and it was the kind of laugh that made the fine hairs rise
on the back of one's neck.

CHAPTER ELEVEN

This was too easy.

Whenever I thought humans had reached the upper reaches of idiocy, they surprised me. Perhaps my little love tap had been too gentle if they were going to send another one down to me.

With the way things were going, I might have to acquire a taste for human flesh. The few times I'd tried it in the Dark Ages, I hadn't cared for it. Too stringy and malodorous. Of course, they didn't move around as much now as they had in the good old days. Perhaps they were tenderer. It was a shame they had to keep sending down the scrawny ones.

"I *knew* it. I knew you were lying to me."

I lashed my tail, using it and my legs to propel me through the water, but it was futile. I'd never been any match for Draugen. She intercepted me before I'd gone a league.

"What is this, a game? You weren't seriously trying to outswim me, Nøkken." She scowled, and I wondered if our years of marriage were going to end rather suddenly, with my poor body torn to pieces.

"Of course not. Why would I try to outswim you? You are my superior in every way, my darling."

"No need to state the obvious. What exactly did you intend to do out here?"

"Nothing, my love. Only out for a wander, checking the territory."

Her nostrils flared. "You *lie*. I caught you, remember? You were watching the humans again. I'll never understand your obsession with them."

Obsessed, me? The very idea was absurd. "I don't know what you're referring to. Are you forgetting that a human-made contraption almost destroyed our home two days ago? I felt it wise to monitor them."

My wife let loose with one of the ultrasonic shrieks she's famous for. My ears popped, and I moved just in time. Her teeth snapped at the exact spot where my tail had been a second before. "I thought you said you chased them away. You were going to take care of them."

"I did, only…in my haste to encourage their leaving, I appear to have damaged their little craft."

Draugen's eyes gleamed in a manner I didn't care for. "You mean they're *stranded*? Here, in our territory?"

"They're going to fix the boat tomorrow, and as soon as it's repaired, they'll be underway. I can assure you, dearheart—they are as good as gone. They certainly won't be coming here again."

"For once you're right, *dear* husband. They won't be coming here, but it has nothing to do with their ridiculous plans. I'm going to take care of this right now."

"Wait." I dove in front of Draugen before she could leave. I knew all too well how my wife took care of things. When she was finished, there wouldn't be enough of that ship left for our son to play with. She would tear the tanker into pieces and kill everyone on board, crunching their skulls between her teeth and leaving a few choice chunks behind for the fish.

"You have one last chance to be honest with me, Nøkken. If you dare lie to me again, the humans die."

"No lies, I promise." I couldn't believe I'd had the temerity to risk my wife's wrath. I hadn't lied to her since before our marriage.

"Why are you so fascinated with this particular group of humans? If it was revenge for wrecking our home, I could understand. But revenge against these creatures is easily exacted. So it must be something else. Tell me what it is that lures you here."

As usual, her questions put me in a perilous position. If I told her the truth about the strange telepathic link I seemed to have with the scientist, my wife would kill me. But if I lied to her, she would kill me anyway. I decided to risk a partial truth.

"This isn't your average tanker, my love. It's a prototype—as small and portable as a drillship, but with minimal crew. They can store oil, but not nearly as much as a tanker. And there are scientists on board."

"Since when are you such an expert?"

Good question. Problem was, I didn't have a very good answer. I had no idea how to describe the link I shared with the scientist, or why my telepathic abilities—usually confined to our own species—had suddenly extended enough to allow me to communicate with a homo sapien.

Draugen rolled her eyes in what I'd come to realize was a typically human gesture. If only she knew.

"Never mind—it doesn't matter. Their level of education doesn't interest me. They're still dumb as sea cucumbers."

"One of the scientists is trying to figure out a means to undo the wrong that's been done by others of her kind. If you destroy her, she won't have the chance to save our home. Or Uisge's home. There will be more humans encroaching on our territory, but they won't be as intelligent or as reasonable, because they'll have heard of the tragedy and will swarm us in an attempt to understand the mystery. Remember poor Uisge."

Draugen sighed, which was always a good sign. "You're right. I forgot what morons they are."

I had stumbled upon the very thing to keep Draugen from slaughtering everyone aboard the ship. If there's anything my wife liked less than humans it was even more humans.

She bared her teeth at me, and it took every ounce of self-control I had not to flee. "What else is going on? I don't think your interest in the humans is confined to their unrealistic ideals. So what is it?"

I should have known I'd never be able to get anything past her. "It's an enjoyable way to spend an afternoon, I suppose, getting involved in their little dramas. You should have seen them today. They nearly…"

"And I suppose your own family isn't entertaining enough for you?"

Uh oh. I scrambled to save face. "It's not that, love. It's only— my cruel streak, you know. I wouldn't want to expose that side of myself to our son."

My wife rolled her eyes again in that endearing, human-like gesture. "Oh Nøkken," she said. "How many times do I have to tell you not to play with your food?"

CHAPTER TWELVE

"What was that?"

The sound of Liam's voice made Flora jump. She whacked her head on one of the bedposts and winced. For a moment, she couldn't remember where she was, and then it came back to her— the creature, Liam's lucky survival, the cuts on his leg, the blood.

She couldn't remember falling asleep, but there was no other explanation for her groggy, confused state. Flora stifled a yawn with her hand. "What was what?"

"Didn't you feel it? I thought the entire ship was going to break." Liam's face glowed a feverish bright pink. She touched his forehead. He was hot, but not unnaturally so.

"It was probably nothing. You were dreaming, most likely."

"That is such bullshit." She'd never heard Liam's voice sound that harsh before. "I know what I felt; I know what I heard, and it certainly wasn't a dream. Wait!" He grabbed her wrist and squeezed. "It's getting closer. Do you know what that means?"

She tried her best to follow, but her brain was fuzzy with sleep. "Please try to relax, Liam. Getting excited like this isn't good for any part of your body, and especially not your leg."

"My leg doesn't matter. Nothing matters." She saw with a shock that he had aged overnight. The happy, carefree Liam she'd grown accustomed to was gone. "Don't you understand? That creature *hates* us. I could feel it. It's going to kill us." He spoke with the weariness of a man three times his age. "We're all going to die, Flora. So it doesn't matter if I lose my leg or not."

Before she could protest, she heard the sound of quick footsteps on the stairs. Her prayers were answered when Thor stuck his tousled head into the cabin.

"How are things going in here? How's our patient?"

Flora made a face she hoped conveyed just how well things were *not* going. "Liam is getting fatalistic on us."

"What? We can't have that. Shove over, dude—seriously."

Groaning, Liam shuffled over on the bed, using his hands to lift and move his injured leg so there was enough room for Thor to sit beside him. For a moment, Flora was horrified and almost yelled at Thor to be careful, but she realized his casual approach was best for Liam, who already looked better than he had a second before. If she were injured, she'd want people to act like nothing had happened too. None of that fawning, sad-faced pity business.

"Your leg's gonna be fine, partner. Frank told me he sewed you together so tight that nothing's getting in there, not even a speck of bacteria. You're all set."

Flora tried to signal him, but it was too late. Liam's face went pale with shock. "*Frank?* I thought Flora was the one who stitched me."

Thor glanced at her in surprise, and she rushed to explain.

"I'm a mess with a needle, remember? I've never been good at that stuff. Frank did a beautiful job. Trust me, you were lucky it was him and not me."

Liam slumped on his pillow, his eyes at half-mast. He shrugged. "Oh well. Guess it doesn't matter what my leg looks like now, anyway."

"It looks great. She's telling you the truth, my friend. He did an awesome job. You probably won't even have much of a scar."

Whatever levity Thor's presence had brought to the little room was gone. Liam turned away from them. "Who cares?" he muttered.

Thor raised an eyebrow at her, and it was her turn to shrug. "Well, I guess *I* care, as much as I can about another fellow's thigh, and Flora cares, and Frank cares. He put a lot of effort into fixing you, you know. The next time you see him, you should thank him."

"I wish he hadn't bothered. He should have let me bleed to death. I'd have preferred that."

Thor's mouth dropped open. It would have been comical if the mood hadn't been so dire. "Preferable to what? What's wrong with you, man? You're lucky to be alive, but I'm not hearing much gratitude from you."

"Liam has decided that we're all going to die," Flora explained.

"Well, that's obvious. We're dying from the day we're born. This is news?"

"He thinks our deaths are more...*imminent* than some. He's convinced the creature is going to return and kill everyone in short order."

"I know you're both laughing at me, but that's only because you weren't there. You haven't seen what I saw, or felt what I felt." Liam pulled the blankets more tightly around his shoulders, as if he longed to bury his head in them. "That creature is determined to kill us, and there's nothing any of us can do to stop it."

"Well, maybe we haven't seen what you have, but as of tomorrow, that should change. That's what I'm hoping, at least," Thor said.

His words were enough to make Liam acknowledge them again. He started to speak, but Flora beat him to it.

"What are you talking about?"

"Whatever is wrong with the ship can't be fixed from the inside." Thor grinned. "I've volunteered to fix it."

"Are you crazy? You've seen what happened to Liam. How can you put yourself at risk that way?" Flora longed to smack that silly smirk off his face. She'd warned them—she'd told them not to let Liam go in the water. And now, after everything that had happened, Thor was going to make the same mistake? *Men.* There was no limit to their idiocy.

"Don't do it, man. It'll kill you." Liam's face was ashen again, and Flora's heart sank. She could have kicked Thor. She still might.

"Nah. We'll be prepared for it this time."

"Prepared? How can you be prepared for this? We don't even know what it is yet," Flora pointed out. Forget kicking. She might start with strangling. What an arrogant man. And here she'd thought Thor was one of the intelligent ones. Perhaps his name gave him delusions of grandeur. She was grateful she hadn't named her own son after a mythological god. Too much to live up to.

"Well, we'll be armed, for one thing."

Liam snorted, and then winced as the movement jostled his injured leg. "With what, rocket launchers?"

"That would be ideal, but unfortunately, we're not a warship. However, we do have harpoon guns." Thor smiled at them. "I'll be armed, and so will the rest of the crew."

"*Everyone's* going into the water? Have you lost your minds?" Flora could feel the blood drain from her face. She wished Thor would move over so she could sit down too. Her legs were feeling a little weak.

"Not that I know of, no. Relax, Flora. I'm going in the water to fix the engine, and the rest of the guys are going to keep watch on deck."

"By the time you see it, it'll be too late. That thing is faster than anything I've ever seen," Liam said.

"It wasn't that fast. We got you out alive, didn't we?"

"Only because it *wanted* you to. It was playing with me, like…like a cat plays with a bird before tearing it apart. Thank God it wasn't in a bad mood, because a lot more than my leg would have been ripped to pieces."

"Oh, come on, man. You can't possibly know that. What are you telling me, that you have some kind of telepathic link with this creature?" Thor rolled his eyes.

"I don't know how I know what it was thinking. I just do. And you're an idiot if you think harpoons are going to stop it. You might as well flick a toothpick at it."

"Harpoon guns kill *whales*, mate. They've taken down the biggest things in the ocean."

"You know that toothpick? That's what a whale would look like next to this thing."

As much as she believed Liam was making a hell of a lot more sense than Thor, Flora had difficulty wrapping her mind around the idea of a creature that large. If it existed, how had it remained hidden for so long? "Wouldn't the sonar have picked up something so huge?"

"Apostolos says it isn't working. I don't know how long it's been down," Thor said.

"Whatever it did to the ship is part of its plan, don't you see? If it wanted to destroy it, it would have ripped it in half by now. It's playing with us. It *wants* someone to try to fix it." Liam's face clouded over. "And the next person who gets in that water isn't coming out."

Thor laughed, giving his friend a gentle punch on the shoulder. Flora noticed he was careful not to bump the man's leg. "Are you hearing yourself? You sound like someone from a horror movie, man. Next thing you'll be telling me we shouldn't separate."

"Not in this case. Best that only one of you has to die before you'll listen to me. Sad it has to be you, though. You were one of the good ones."

The smile left Thor's face, and Flora knew why. There was something about the certainty in Liam's voice. He had no doubt Thor was going to die the next day, and he was beginning to convince her. She shivered.

Thor grimaced. "I don't know about you two, but I'd rather take my chances with some sea monster, which may or may not even be around tomorrow—"

"It'll be there. This is like a sport for it," Liam interrupted.

"—than with starvation, which is a sure thing. We can't drift about on the ocean forever, boys and girls. Sooner or later, we're going to need supplies. We need to get this baby fixed, and only three people can do that. One of them is lying in this bed."

"Can't another ship tow us in?" Flora asked. "There has to be an alternative."

Thor shook his head. "Apostolos says the radio hasn't been working since the engine got pooched. There's a chance our first distress call went through, but he doesn't want to wait around and see. And I agree with him." A beseeching expression came over his face. "This is something I can do to help. Frank did a great job with Liam's leg—I'm not saying he didn't—but Liam still needs professional care. We need to get him to a hospital, and the sooner the better."

Finally something she couldn't argue with. She hadn't liked the look of Liam's wounds, and she didn't like the way he was acting now. She wasn't a doctor—what if he *did* have a fever? What if it was broiling his brain?

"Don't risk your life on my account," Liam said. "I don't want anyone's blood on my hands."

"No one's life is being risked. I'll be armed tomorrow, and the second I see something I don't like, I'll shoot the hell out of it."

"I'm going to sleep now. I'm tired of talking. But if you're going to keep being idiotic, you should at least see what you're dealing with. Check out those photos I shot this afternoon and then tell me how effective you think your little harpoon gun is going to be."

Flora felt like she'd been struck, and she could tell from the expression on Thor's face that he felt the same.

The camera.

They'd forgotten all about it.

CHAPTER THIRTEEN

It took him forever to find the damn thing, and in searching for it, he almost destroyed it. Thor lifted his boot just in time.

"Flora." He whispered her name into the darkness, not wanting to alert the other guys, but he needn't have worried. From what he could hear from the messdeck, the party had really started after he'd left. Perhaps Liam was right. Thor didn't feel comfortable leaving his safety in the hands of a bunch of drunken morons. Or hungover ones, for that matter.

Flora's flashlight turned toward him. He winced, holding out a hand to block the beam.

"Did you find it?"

"Yeah, I've got it. Nearly stepped on it."

"Great. Let's get out of here. This place gives me the creeps." She hurried to his side, which surprised him. She wasn't a damsel-in-distress type.

He was tempted to point out that 'this place' was the deck of the ship, and that there was nothing creepy about fresh air and a sky full of stars. If she wanted creepy, she'd already had her fill with Liam, whose injury had apparently turned him into Rod Serling and Nostradamus rolled into one.

It was if she'd read his mind. "What? What did I say?"

"Nothing. It's only…we're outside on the deck. What's creepy about it?"

"I don't know." Flora stared at the sky, tilting her head until her dark curls tumbled over her shoulders. "Maybe it's how dark it is. I'm not used to it being so dark."

"You like your stars with a little light pollution?" He bumped her shoulder so she'd know he wasn't laughing *at* her. "That's actually one of the things I love about being at sea—you can really see the stars out here. Sometimes I sleep on the deck."

She shivered. "You couldn't pay me enough to sleep out here."

"What's going on, Flora? What's bugging you? Is it Liam? I realize he's acting strange, but that's to be expected after what he's been through."

Rubbing her arms, she stared at the ocean, which was a flat, wide expanse of black. Once more it was eerily calm. Not a whitecap to be seen. The ship rarely moved under their feet; it was so steady it could have been docked. "I don't know. Maybe it's only Liam's influence, but for a few days, I've felt different whenever I'm out here. I hate to use the word *evil*, because that's a tad dramatic, but whatever I'm feeling isn't good. Whenever I'm on deck, I feel like I'm not alone, and not in a good way. Something is listening to me. Something is watching. Don't you feel it?"

Thor would be the first to admit he wasn't the most imaginative guy, but he understood exactly what she was getting at. In the last couple days—ever since the drill string had been destroyed—the air had acquired a strange weight. It was heavy, as if the universe was holding its breath, waiting for something. A chill ran over his spine, making his skin feel like spiders were crawling on it. He laughed again to hide his nerves. "Now you're giving *me* the creeps. Let's go see Liam's monster, shall we?"

He linked arms with Flora, and they were almost at the stairs when he turned to face the ocean again. He didn't know what made him do it—it was some kind of compulsion, he guessed—but he waved at the ocean like an idiot. "Bye, monster. See you tomorrow."

"Don't do that." Flora hissed the words at him through clenched teeth, yanking his sleeve. The fabric cut into his arm, pinching his wrist.

"Aw, relax, will ya? I was just joking around." He already regretted what he'd said. If the atmosphere on the ship had been heavy before, now it threatened to crush them.

"How can you joke about it? Liam's nearly dead from blood loss and shock, and you're about to subject yourself to the same thing. How can you possibly find this funny?"

The disappointment in her voice shamed him. He didn't want her to think he was as big a jerk as the rest of the guys.

"Sorry, I was trying to lighten the mood. It's a bad habit with me. I do it whenever I'm nervous."

"Try not to do it again. Whatever's down there didn't like it."

"Are you serious about this, Flora? Do you really think they're sentient beings who are listening to every word we say?"

She glanced over her shoulder, and he could see sweat beading her forehead, though the evening was cool. "Yes. I know it sounds crazy, but I do. I feel like everything I say here is heard—and not only heard, but evaluated, as if I'm constantly being judged. Do you know what I mean?"

Thor didn't like where the discussion was going. The more she talked, the more sense she made, and he didn't want to think of the creature that way. It wasn't capable of intelligent thought. It was only a dumb animal, no matter how extraordinary its existence may be. He had to think of it like that. If he began to believe Flora's point of view, there would be no way in hell he'd have the guts to get in the water tomorrow morning.

* * *

When they got to the cabin, Liam was asleep. Or perhaps he'd passed out. It was difficult to tell.

They tiptoed past the messdeck, where the Neanderthals were laughing louder than ever. It pissed him off. For one, they'd no doubt finished Thor's share of the beer by now. For another, it would have been considerate for at least one of them to stay sober, seeing as he was putting his ass on the line for them in the morning. He'd be surprised if anyone was able to stand upright tomorrow, let alone shoot straight.

He couldn't keep pretending Liam was going to be fine. The man's face was covered in ugly red splotches and his breathing was ragged. "What's wrong with him?" Thor asked, before realizing what a dumb question that was.

Flora rushed to Liam's side and touched his forehead.

"His skin is on fire. I think infection is setting in. Can you find me some painkillers?"

"I've got some aspirin in my bag."

"No, it has to be ibuprofen or Tylenol. Would anyone else have something like that?"

"I could ask, but I doubt I'd get a coherent answer," he said, as another burst of raucous laughter shook the walls. Making up his mind, he walked to Frank's bunk and pulled down the sailor's duffel bag.

"What are you doing?"

"What does it look like?" He unbuttoned the outside pockets and undid the straps. "I'm finding you some painkillers."

"But shouldn't you ask first? Won't the guys be mad if they find out you went through their stuff?"

"Hey, if I thought they were capable of rational thought right now, I'd ask. Do you want the pills or not?"

Flora stopped protesting, and he was glad. The last thing he needed was another conscience. Pawing through another guy's things was against the sailors' code. Technically, most of the men weren't sailors, but since they lived on a ship, following the code was the best way to make it home in one piece.

Not that this crew had much to hide. A flask of whiskey in Archie's bag (rotgut by the smell of it), a bit of weed and some girly mags in Frank's (Thor was glad he wasn't the one cleaning the sheets), and photographs of a woman with a sweet, lovely face in George's. George, a softy? Who knew? It was in George's bag Thor found the Tylenol, which he tossed to Flora. She whipped out a Swiss Army knife and crushed four of the tablets with the flat of the blade before mixing the powder with some water.

"Can you help me?" she whispered. "Someone needs to hold his head."

He had no idea why she was whispering, since Liam was dead to the world and the other guys certainly couldn't hear them, but there wasn't time to ask. She was already tilting the foul concoction toward Liam's mouth.

Lifting the engineer's head as gently as he could, Thor was shocked by the heat of his skin. Liam's hair was damp with sweat.

"Liam?" Flora took hold of his arm, shaking it gently. "Liam, you have to drink this. Please open your mouth."

The poor bastard was clearly not happy about being awake, and Thor couldn't blame him. Sleeping was probably Liam's only escape from the pain, going by the way he thrashed and moaned.

As Flora forced the cup to his mouth, Thor noticed his lips were chapped and blistered. Half of the drugged water ran down his chin and soaked his shirt, but she seemed satisfied with how much Liam had managed to drink. Thor settled his head on the pillow again.

"Something isn't right. He's really sick," he said. He couldn't understand how Liam's condition had deteriorated this much in the few minutes they'd been on deck. Had he done something desperate to hasten the demise he was so fond of talking about?

"We should get some ice. For his head. Cool him down a little. He must be uncomfortable."

They both looked at the ceiling, toward the messdeck. Thor figured he could read her mind—she didn't want to go there and deal with the rest of the crew, and no wonder. Most of them got along fine with him, and he didn't want to go there either.

He was surprised to see Flora unwind the blanket from Liam's body, exposing his bare legs. "What are you doing?"

"Shh...I have to check his wound."

As soon as the blanket was pulled aside, she clapped a hand over her mouth and nose, stifling a retch. The room was filled with a sweet, sickening stench that made Thor's gorge rise.

"Jesus Christ—what's that smell?"

Still holding her nose, Flora pointed at Liam's wound. Between the stitches, the skin looked even angrier and redder than before. But even worse was the pus. Every wound was weeping a sickly yellow fluid.

"Fuck."

"Go get Frank," she said, giving him a little shove. "And please hurry."

Fuck fuck fuck. He didn't need a medic to give him the bad news, and he knew from Flora's expression that she didn't, either.

Liam's dire prediction was coming true.

* * *

The men's voices stopped the second Thor appeared in the messdeck, which made him suspicious. Had they been talking about him? And if so, what could they possibly have to say that they wouldn't feel comfortable saying to his face? It wasn't like they were a crew of meek gentlemen.

He cleared his throat, forcing himself to speak over the lump that was wedged in the middle of it. "Frank, we need you below."

Frank's nose was bright red, with ugly purple veins Thor had never noticed before. The sailor blinked at him. "What do you want? I'm taking a break. It's not my shift yet."

"There's something wrong with Liam."

The sailor laughed. It was a hideous sound, as ugly as the veins on his nose. "Of course there's something wrong with him. That boy is lucky to still have a leg."

Thor had to yell to be heard over the chorus of responding roars. "This is something else. He's got a fever, and some gross stuff coming out of his wounds. And he reeks. He's stinking up the room."

Frank grumbled in response, but Thor was relieved when he pushed his chair away from the table and stood, however unsteadily. "Probably shit himself. Surely you can change a diaper without my help."

"It isn't that, Frank. This is something with his leg. I'm not a doctor, but it looks pretty bad to me."

"No, you're not a doctor. If you were, you'd know not to disturb one when he's on a break."

The other men roared with laughter again, but Thor noticed Apostolos didn't join in this time. Frowning, the big Greek followed them down the stairs. "I have some first-aid training. Maybe I can help."

The smell had gotten worse in the few minutes Thor'd been away. By the time they'd made it halfway down the stairs, the stench hit them.

Frank staggered, pulling his arm across his face. He glowered at Thor. "Jesus Christ, man. What took you so long to come get me?"

"It wasn't that bad before. Hell, it wasn't this bad a minute ago."

The men rushed down the stairs so fast Thor worried one of them would fall and break something. Frank hurried to the door and stopped short, coughing. When he looked at Thor, his eyes were watery. "Jesus Christ, man," he repeated. "This isn't right."

If possible, the smell was even more powerful than before. Flora crouched in the corner of the room, clutching a small metal trashcan. "I-I'm sorry," she said. "I puked. I couldn't help it."

"No one's gonna blame you for that." Frank straightened his shoulders and marched over to the bed. The stink rolled off Liam in noxious waves. Thankfully, the man was unconscious. He thrashed his head from side to side, muttering. Someone—most likely Flora, as Thor didn't think Liam was in any state to do it himself—had re-covered his leg with the blanket.

Now that Thor was closer, he could hear an ominous sizzling noise coming from Liam, like bacon on a grill.

"What in the blue blazes of hell…?" Frank whipped the blanket off Liam's body.

Thor cried out. Actually, if he were to be honest, he screamed like a bloody girl, but he couldn't help it.

The men stared at Liam's femur. All of the flesh, the healthy muscle and skin, was gone. Even Frank's threadwork had disappeared. It was clear where the sizzling noise was coming from. As they watched, horrified, an oozing liquid fizzled around the base of Liam's knee. The skin around his kneecap was dissolving.

"Quick, help me lift him. We have to get him to the shower, wash this stuff off," Frank said.

Thor held Liam's shoulders while Frank took his legs, extra careful to keep his hands away from that strangely fizzing liquid. When they touched his leg, Liam shrieked and promptly passed out again. Thor's eyes filled with tears.

"Wait," Flora said as they muscled what was left of their friend's leg into the shower. Liam face was a sickly shade of gray, and Thor feared they didn't have long. "Do you really want to wash that stuff down the drain? What if it corrodes the plumbing?"

"Then we'll do without some showers, you selfish bitch," Frank replied, turning the water on full blast. As it hit his bones, Liam's eyes flew open. Thor tried to keep him from seeing his leg, but he was too slow. Liam started screaming and didn't stop.

Thor had never heard a man in so much anguish. He wanted nothing more than to run to the deck, or grab a few beers in the messdeck and get himself properly pissed. Frank caught his gaze and shook his head. So Thor tried his best to hold Liam still, leaning on the man's chest as he thrashed and hollered.

The screaming brought the other men downstairs fast. They sounded like they were tripping over each other as they pounded down the stairs. Clustering around the tiny bathroom, they were held at bay by the terrible smell and Liam's shrieking, which was ear shattering in the enclosed space.

Thor's stomach churned, and he took deep breaths from his mouth, hoping he could avoid throwing up.

"Holy fuck. What the hell happened?" George cried. Thor couldn't risk turning to look at him, but recognized the man's voice, which was thick with emotion and alcohol.

"We don't know," Frank said, and Thor saw the sailor's hands were shaking where he held what was left of Liam's leg.

A heavy *clunk* plunged them into silence. Blood—great crimson swirls of it—began to run down the drain. Liam's leg had detached at the knee.

When Frank realized he was holding a sizzling calf no longer attached to Liam, he jumped, tossing the bone on the floor. Apostolos shoved past him, ripping off his own shirt, which he wrapped around Liam's upper thigh and hip to staunch the blood. Sweat and water poured down his face as he applied pressure to Liam's lower body. Frank slumped against the toilet seat, panting.

Thor focused on Liam's face rather than watch whatever was consuming him from the inside out. The younger man was quiet now. His skin had lost that terrible gray color and appeared normal again. Thor put his hand to Liam's mouth but felt nothing. Refusing to believe it, he pressed two fingers to his neck. The result was the same.

"He's gone."

"What do you mean, *gone*? He can't be gone. He just had a few cuts on his leg." Apostolos's tone was accusatory, but Thor tried not to take it personally.

"I think it was more than a few cuts, boss," Archie said from the doorway. He pointed to Liam's thigh, which was now nearly bone as well.

Thor wasn't sure how long he sat with the water splashing his face and Liam's head in his lap, but eventually George lifted him to his feet. The men slept on deck that night. No one could stand the smell in the cabin.

CHAPTER FOURTEEN

There are no glossy photos of proud fishermen standing beside our kin with triumphant grins on their faces. Even if one did manage to catch us, his fate would be sealed the moment he touched us.

There are fish that can feed on our blood, or our carcasses, if they're fortunate enough to come across one before it dissolves, but most marine creatures keep their distance. Which is fine with us.

I felt guilty about killing the young man. It had never been my intention. He'd zigged when I zagged, that was all. If he hadn't been set on taking those ridiculous photographs, he'd most likely still be alive. He would have scaled that rope and been on board before my tail whipped around and caught him.

Heaving a sigh, I forced the incident out of my mind. What's done is done, and it wasn't like the man's death would cause a population shortage. I could devour entire continents of people, most of the planet even, before they'd need to get concerned about their species' survival.

However, I'd seen how personally humans took everything, and I did not doubt I would be blamed for the man's death, even though technically it wasn't my fault. Pretty soon, they'd be hauling out the pitchforks and torches, or the harpoon guns, as it were. There was no reasoning with them. They didn't appear to possess a wit of logic. Stubborn fools.

"I don't understand why you care what they think of you," my wife said when she noticed my glum mood. "We were here long before them, and we'll be here after them. Their little whims and notions are nothing to us."

"Did you hear what they called us? *Monsters.* A monster is an imaginary creature that's large, ugly, and frightening. It's insulting."

Draugen laughed. "You're proving my point. See what little they know? If we were imaginary, we wouldn't be here, would we? I resent the inference that we're something the human mind conjured up." She shuddered theatrically. "And we're far from ugly. If you ask me, humans are the ugly ones, with their tiny yellow teeth and their beady eyes. That pink, raw flesh and runny red blood—ick. They're disgusting."

"I think they may have a different standard of beauty than us," I said, although as much as I'd observed the humans, I hadn't been able to figure out what it was. I'd always thought my wife was beautiful, even when she was threatening to kill me—she was lovely in her rage, to be sure—but I could see why humans might think otherwise. They would probably find the sight of her terrifying.

"Pah. A fish has more sense." She glided around the room at a speed that warned of her rising temper. So I didn't bother to argue, although privately I disagreed. I didn't think fish had any sense, period. These are the same creatures that swim directly into nets, or see a shiny metal hook and think it's something good to eat.

"Can I bring the little boat down here today, so we can be done with this? Our son needs a new toy for his collection, and you know he's never had a drillship. He'll be thrilled."

I thought of the humans, who were in the process of wrapping their friend's body—or what was left of it—in blankets. They planned to store him in the cargo hold until they could get home and present the corpse to the man's mother. Strange practice, that. The sailors of old simply dumped the bodies into the sea, where they could be food for other organisms.

I wish I could have told them it was useless.

It had been easier to keep track of the humans when the engineer was still alive. As long as some of my essence flowed through his brain, I had been privy to his thoughts, as well as everything that was said and done around him. With him gone, all I had was my link to the female geologist, and I wasn't sure how strong that was or how long it would last. I'd have to risk going near the surface again to keep a proper eye on what they were doing.

"Let's give him the ship for his millennium," I said. "We shouldn't keep giving him gifts for no reason, or he'll get spoiled. He's already getting quite willful, don't you think?"

Willful was a colossal understatement, but I knew Draugen wouldn't stand for much criticism of our son. The only reason he minded me was that he knew I could kill him quite easily. (He probably also knew I'd considered it several times, Draugen be damned.)

At some point during the day, she'd swam through a kelp bed, and the strands waved around her face like hair when she tossed her head. "I suppose you're right. He has been rather difficult lately. But I want this to be over soon, Nøkken. No more obsessing over the humans."

Before I rose to the surface, I gave her my word.

It would be over soon, one way or another.

There was no doubt about that.

CHAPTER FIFTEEN

After Liam's death, everyone spent a lot more time on deck. No one could bear to return to the cabin, which still reeked, even though the men had thrown the soiled bedding overboard.

Flora didn't like being out in the open air. She preferred her cabin, in spite of the fact it had taken on some of the same horrible smell. When she was on deck, she didn't feel safe, but she kept this to herself. Ever since the engineer had died, the mood toward her—always unfriendly—had grown hostile. She stuck close to Thor, the only guy she had some camaraderie with. The one good thing that resulted from the sad incident with Liam was that it had delayed Thor's attempt to repair the ship.

Not surprisingly, Apostolos wasn't keen to send one of his best men into the ocean.

Flora tried to avoid the big Greek and the other men whenever possible, but it wasn't easy. She grabbed a quick sandwich after the rest of the crew had finished eating, scurrying in and out of the messdeck like a mouse. After a couple of days, she was tired of hiding. She hadn't done anything wrong. Maybe they would always treat her like a leper, but she wasn't going to help them do it anymore.

As soon as she heard the scraping of several chairs being pulled away from the table, she went downstairs to join the others. The boisterous laughter stopped when she entered. Thor raised an eyebrow at her, but he indicated the chair beside him.

Frank knocked his hand away. "Don't bother, son. She's not welcome here."

Flora's cheeks grew hot. "What do you mean, I'm not welcome here?" She could hear her voice shaking, and took a deep breath to steady it. "I'm still part of this crew."

The gruff man snorted. "You've never been part of this crew. We don't have any use for a goddamn Jonah."

"Maybe you should go, Duchovney," Apostolos said in a gentle tone that made her even angrier. The last thing she needed from the big Greek was pity. "We don't want any trouble here."

"I'm not going anywhere. You guys have been avoiding me ever since Liam died. I have a right to know why you're blaming me. I haven't done anything wrong." Tears of frustration stung her eyes, but she forced them back. She wouldn't give any of those bastards the satisfaction of seeing her cry.

George lunged from the table, a dangerous expression on his face, but Archie and Thor seized his arms.

"I think you should go, Flora. I'll bring you something later, okay? Maybe wait for me on deck," Thor said, and she could see the warning in his eyes. She knew he didn't mean to reject her, but his words hurt more than anything else.

"Okay, fine. But I don't understand why I'm suddenly not welcome to have a sandwich with you."

"Are you completely obtuse, woman?" Frank hollered, banging his fist on the table hard enough that the cutlery clattered. "You busted our drill string, wrecked our ship, and killed Liam. You're a bloody Jonah. If this was the Middle Ages, someone would have burned you at the stake by now."

The color drained from Flora's face, and she groped for the handrail for support. "What—I don't—"

"She wasn't to blame for any of those things, Frank," Thor said in a calm voice. He put a hand on the man's shoulder, but Frank shook him off.

"The hell she wasn't. You're thinking with the wrong head, Anderssen. The rest of us can see her clearly. She's bad luck, is what she is."

"What are you talking about? I didn't kill Liam—I took care of him while the rest of you were here getting drunk." Flora was gratified to hear new strength in her voice.

"You made him get in the water," George said, rising from his chair again. His eyes were red-rimmed. "You, with your ridiculous stories of sea creatures and supernatural bullshit."

"I did *not* make him go in the water. I tried to talk him out of it. Thor was there. Thor, please tell him the truth." She looked at her friend in desperation.

"I've tried, but they won't believe me. They've got it in their heads that you're responsible for what happened to Liam, and they won't listen to anything different," Thor said. "Guys, if anyone talked Liam into doing what he did, it was me. Flora thought it was a bad idea from the start. Unfortunately, neither of us listened to her."

"Guess who's thinking with his dick again," Frank said to a general murmur of assent.

Flora glared at the sailor. "I am *not* sleeping with Thor. How can you accuse me of these things? How can you think I had anything to do with Liam's death? I tried to save him, but I'm not a doctor. I did the best I could."

She couldn't close her eyes without seeing the young man thrashing on his pus-soaked bed, out of his mind with pain. She had nightmares where the flesh dissolved from the man's bones again and her ears were filled with that terrible sizzling.

"You shouldn't have given him the Tylenol."

For a moment, she wasn't sure she had heard the sailor right. "He had a fever, Frank. You really think giving him Tylenol is what caused his skin to dissolve?"

The man shrugged. He still wouldn't meet her eyes, which she knew was a bad sign. The more the crew depersonalized her, the easier it would be to hate her.

It was George who answered.

"He was fine until you gave him those pills. *Fine.* You came along and everything went to hell. Frank was his doctor. You should have asked him what to do. You should have never given Liam nothing without Frank's say-so."

"Frank wasn't there to ask. He was in here getting pissed."

This time, both George and Frank lunged at her, and it took everything the other men had to hold them.

"What are you going to do, hit me? Would hitting a woman do it for you? Would that solve things?"

"I wouldn't bother hitting ya, witch. I'd throw you overboard," Frank said, and the cruelty in his eyes made her shudder.

"Duchovney, as your supervisor, I'm ordering you to leave this room and go on deck," Apostolos said. "Thor will bring you your lunch."

She knew she should keep her mouth shut, but she had her pride. "You haven't been my supervisor since the day you said you were firing me."

The Greek sighed heavily. "I'm still the captain of this boat, and I'm responsible for every soul on it. I'm telling you this for your own good—leave this room. That's an order."

Flora's chin trembled, and she knew her emotions wouldn't be kept in check much longer. "Fine. I'll go. You can have your scapegoat. But I want you to know I cared about Liam. I did everything I could to save him." She surveyed the men at the table, all of whom refused to look at her. Even Thor had bowed his head. "I did a hell of a lot more to help him than any of you."

"Go." Apostolos pointed at the stairs.

She did, taking her time, ascending each stair deliberately. The tears didn't fall until she was alone.

* * *

An hour later, Thor arrived with her lunch.

"How are you feeling?"

"What do you think? How could they say those things? How could they think them? I didn't have anything to do with Liam's death."

"I know that, and you know that, but I guess they need someone to lash out at." He shrugged, setting down a plate that had a roast beef sandwich and a pickle on it. "Some of the guys believe that old superstition that women are bad luck on a ship. It's ridiculous."

"It's more than ridiculous—it's scary. It's getting so I feel safer taking my chances with the creature. What if they do something to hurt me? What if they really do throw me overboard?"

"Don't worry. Nothing's going to happen to you. Apostolos won't let them touch you, and neither will I. You're just going to have to keep your distance until we land," Thor said, his voice heavy with regret. "I'm sorry, but I'll bring you your lunch and dinner every day, I promise. I can even make you something special, if you like—tell me what you want, and I'll make it happen."

"If Apostolos won't let them hurt me, why do I have to keep my distance?"

"Just because a lion is in a cage doesn't mean you should poke it with a stick. The men are angry right now, and angry men are unpredictable. I think even the Greek is nervous about the potential for violence. Maybe if they don't see you for a while, they'll calm down."

She brushed new tears from her eyes and stared at the ocean. It was still flat and calm, like it had been since the day the drill string was destroyed. She'd always loved the ocean, was ordinarily soothed by it, but no more. Now she hated it with a passion. If she ever got home, it would be a long, dark day before she went near the water again.

Thor touched her shoulder. "I'm really sorry. I did try to reason with them, but it didn't do any good. They think I'm biased."

"I know. I heard." He was so young—not much older than Liam. Just a kid, really. The only people keeping her alive were a kid and a boss who loathed her. It was less than comforting. "Let me ask you a question. Do you think the Tylenol killed Liam?"

"Of course not. Even if he were allergic to it, it wouldn't have caused that kind of reaction. I think something got into his wounds from that—that *thing* out there, whatever it is. Maybe some sort of toxin. It dissolved Liam's flesh and killed him— everyone saw it happen. I don't think the Tylenol had anything to do with it."

She exhaled in relief. Until that moment, she hadn't realized she'd been holding her breath. "Thank you."

"No need to thank me. I'm only calling 'em as I see 'em, and I told the guys the same. Hey—I brought something that might make you feel better."

Flora eyed the sandwich. Thor had obviously taken some time to make it for her, but she'd lost her appetite after the confrontation in the messdeck. "I'm sorry, Thor—it looks great, but I'm not hungry right now. Maybe later."

He grinned. "I'm not talking about the sandwich. Remember this?" Thor pulled a small waterproof camera out of his pocket.

She felt her heart beat a little faster. "Liam's pictures."

"Yeah, we forgot about them after…what happened. I haven't gone through them yet. Why don't we do that together?"

"As long as we stay here. I don't want to deal with anyone else right now."

"Don't worry—no one's going to bother us. Apostolos made them promise."

She was still nervous, but Thor was correct—the photographs were a welcome distraction. Perhaps Liam had gotten a shot good enough for her to identify the creature. And if she could identify it, that would be the first step in fighting it.

They sat down on the wooden planking of the deck, the sun warm on their heads. The hours spent outside had darkened her skin until she was as olive-toned as Apostolos. Thor, with his Scandinavian heritage, wasn't as lucky. He was trapped in a perpetual cycle of burning and peeling. At least he'd started to wear a ball cap to shield his face, which made him look even younger.

She felt her pulse quicken as Thor hit the power button, bringing the camera to life. For a moment, she was afraid the battery would be dead, or the pictures would be destroyed from the rough treatment the camera had received.

But her fears were for naught. Thor quickly cycled through the photos, most of which showed indistinct, watery blobs.

"Wait…go back," Flora said, leaning closer. "What's that?"

This particular picture showed a blob with a bit more shape.

Thor squinted at the photo. "I can't tell. Doesn't look like much to me. I think that's just the side of the ship."

"No, no…this is shaped kind of like a snake, see?" She tapped the screen with a fingernail. "And look at this. Could that be a fin, maybe?"

"You have more imagination than me. I can't see anything but a blob."

"Maybe I'm reaching. I probably want to see something too much. Let's move on to the next one."

Thor advanced to the next frame, and Flora clapped her hand to her mouth.

"My God..."

The photo was full of teeth. Giant teeth. Fangs, exposed in a—*could it be?*—grin. There was a bit of nostril, but mostly teeth. The side of the boat, visible at the far edge of the frame, was toy-sized next to the creature. They wouldn't stand a chance against it, even if they stayed on the ship.

The rational side of her struggled to regain control. The existence of a marine animal that large was simply not possible. Where would it live? What did it eat? And why had it never been spotted before? It was too massive to hide for long, even in the ocean.

No, the camera must have distorted the creature's size. Nothing was that gigantic, not even the great whales.

Thor continued to study the picture. It didn't appear to unnerve him in the same way. "Leviathan..." he breathed.

She shuddered. "The biblical serpent?"

"Hey, some people think it really exists. It makes sense if there's a factual basis for these ancient stories. What if this was what people were referring to when they wrote about Leviathan?"

"I don't believe in biblical serpents any more than Noah's magic ark. I'm a scientist, remember? Bible stories are closer to mythology than fact."

Thor raised an eyebrow, nudging her with the camera. "What does your scientific education have to say about this?"

"There's always an explanation. Just because we don't happen to know it doesn't mean there isn't one."

"Come on, Flora—you're an oceanographer. You have training in marine biology. This is your field of study. Have you ever seen anything like it?"

She forced herself to examine the photo even though it horrified her. *It's only an animal, silly. And a picture of it, at that. Nothing to be afraid of.* But no matter how she tried to reason with herself, she still felt like something was listening—waiting for her opinion, as if a lot was riding on her next few words. She shifted on the deck, flexing her feet to alleviate the pins and needles.

"At first glance, the teeth are snakelike, but there are too many of them. A snake's teeth are spaced few and far between, and most don't have that many. This creature's mouth is full of them." Flora thought for a moment. "It's unlikely, but this could still be a type of water snake I'm not familiar with. Mammals were my specialty. I don't know that much about reptiles."

"Are you shitting me? A water snake? Do you see how huge that thing is?" He shook his head. "No snake is that big. It's not possible."

"I think the angle of the picture distorts the size. Because it was taken at such close range, the creature might be a lot smaller."

The ship groaned loudly in response, shifting from side to side, as if something massive passed underneath it.

"Do you really believe that, Flora?" Thor's hazel eyes dared her to lie to him.

"No, I don't. But I can't handle the reality of this."

The Cormorant moaned again, and as Apostolos hurried onto the deck, they stumbled to their feet. "What's that sound?" the Greek asked, peering over the edge of the ship. "What's happening?"

"It could be the creature swimming underneath us. I think it knocked something loose the last time."

Apostolos whirled on Thor. "How many times do I have to tell you? Liam's death was an accident. What happened to the ship was an accident. There is no creature."

Steeling herself, Flora wedged her body between them. She refused to let this man push her around any longer. She hadn't been to blame for the horrible things that had befallen *The Cormorant*, and damned if she would take his abuse in silence any longer.

"Yes, there is. And we have proof."

CHAPTER SIXTEEN

Thor suspected Flora thought the pictures would change things. And maybe he'd hoped the same, but if he'd thought about it a bit longer, he could have predicted the outcome.

If anything, the guys were even more eager to fix *The Cormorant* and move into safer waters.

One thing *did* change. Liam's photos caused such a ruckus that no one said a word when Flora started joining them in the messdeck again. She was quiet for the most part, but when she had something to say, the guys listened. Maybe they finally realized she knew more about this kind of thing than the rest of them combined. The crew's only encounters with marine life thus far had been catching a few fish or some lobsters for dinner. That hardly prepared anyone for this.

"Are you still willing to go below, Anderssen?"

Thor could tell Apostolos hoped he would refuse. The captain didn't want to wrap someone else's remains in a towel and store them in the cargo hold beside Liam's. But Thor knew he was the only option. None of the others had his mechanical knowledge—Apostolos might know more about the ship, but he was the captain. The Greek couldn't sacrifice himself.

"Yes. We have to fix the ship, and it has to be done from below. The radio isn't working. We haven't seen another craft in days. If we don't get this barge working, we'll starve." Thor prayed he'd be able to fix *The Cormorant* before he was ripped to shreds.

"Watch it," Archie said, patting the table. "Ships are sensitive. She has feelings, you know." No one smiled.

"Let's get it over with, then. Could you be ready in an hour?" Apostolos asked.

"That's more than enough time. I just need to suit up, and then I'll meet everyone on deck."

"I'll have to get the harpoon guns sorted. Obviously I wasn't prepared for this kind of situation. So take an hour. Duchovney?"

"Yes?" She sounded surprised. Thor was grateful the other men could now hear her voice without snarling.

"What do you think our chances are?"

"Honestly?"

When Apostolos nodded, she continued, watching the men around the table as if afraid someone would pounce. Thor understood her anxiety, but was sad she was still so nervous. During the first week of the job, they'd been such a tight-knit group. They weren't used to having a woman on the crew, but it had been a nice change. He'd never expected things to get so ugly.

"I think you're sending Thor to his death. Based on our best guess, this creature is gigantic—several times bigger than the largest whale known to man. Harpoons may distract it temporarily, but they'll probably make it angrier. We don't have a chance of stopping something this massive."

"So what do you suggest?" Archie asked. "We have to get the ship fixed. You heard Anderssen—we're running out of time."

"Thankfully, we were planning to drill, so we have at least a few weeks of supplies left before we have to start worrying," said Apostolos. "And as long as you fools keep filling your stomachs with beer instead of food, we won't have to ration for quite a while."

"I think the one thing that might work is a distraction. Whatever we have on board that a creature like that would want, we should throw it off the bow as you guys lower Thor off the stern," Archie said. "Depending on the quantity of food we have to spare, it would buy us a little time." He turned to Thor. "How much do you think you'll need?"

Thor shrugged, unable to believe how subdued everyone was. Ordinarily it was difficult to get a word in without another man cutting him off. "Hard to say. I can't diagnose the problem until I'm down there, but I'm thinking something might have gotten dislodged when the creature swam underneath us. Hopefully we don't need a new part."

"Sorry, but throwing food in the water is a bad idea. If it does draw the creature, it'll be able to see everything we're doing. Remember, there is no bow or stern as far as it's concerned—if it's as large as we think, it dwarfs the ship."

"I never thought I'd say this, but I agree with Flora. Never mind the fact that throwing our supplies overboard would be suicide," Frank said.

"Well…what about Liam? We could use his body," Archie said, and George shifted in his chair.

"Liam was our friend. No one is throwing him overboard for that—that *monster*."

Archie held up a hand. "Sorry, it was only a suggestion. He's dead now—it's not like he can feel anything."

"It wouldn't work, anyway. There's nothing left."

The room grew quiet again. Everyone stared at the Greek, waiting for him to explain. "I checked on him this morning. He's gone. All that's left is a bit of bone."

"That's sick. Who would take his body?" George turned on Flora. "You touched him, didn't you, witch?"

"Of course I didn't touch him. Why would I—?"

"Quiet down, all of you." Apostolos glowered around the table until he had everyone's attention. "George, I don't think anyone took him. What was already happening to him…well, it finished the job, I guess."

George collapsed in his chair, holding his big head in his hands.

"What would a thing like this eat?" Apostolos asked Flora.

"I-I'm not sure. I've never seen anything like this before," she said. "But judging by its teeth, I'd guess it's a carnivore."

"We don't have much meat on board in any case," Apostolos said. "It's the first thing we'll run out of—that and the booze." He rolled his eyes. "Big surprise there. Anything else you can think of?"

"Well, this is just a theory—it's not based on anything concrete. It's more of a hunch than anything." Flora hesitated, but no one argued with her. If anyone was prepared to believe in hunches, it was a sailor. "I don't think the creature is around us all the time. I suspect it goes to its home—wherever that may be—in the evening. So that's probably the best time to fix the ship."

Apostolos raised an eyebrow at Thor. "You okay with that, Anderssen?"

"As long as the lamps keep working, I'm fine."

He was lying, of course. The last place he wanted to be was in the dark ocean with that God-knows-what swimming around.

CHAPTER SEVENTEEN

You have to wonder about a creature that sees monsters everywhere it looks.

Carnivore, indeed.

I admit the teeth are a tad misleading. They're a holdover from the days when our primary diet was meat, but unlike the humans, we could tell when it was time to diversify. If we'd continued to feast on other animals at the same rate, there wouldn't be another living thing in the ocean. And eventually our kind would have perished as well.

Not to mention the ethical concerns of eating other creatures. We're not cannibals, and whales, while not exactly kin, are close enough that we can understand each other's languages. It's difficult to eat something with a clear conscience when you can hear it pleading for its life. The occasional shark is acceptable, albeit not very filling, but the humans have done such a number on them that we try to avoid culling them even further. Someone has to show them some compassion, and it might as well be us. Although my son wasn't happy about this—he'd grown fond of snacking on sharks, especially the big whites. He liked to string their teeth for a necklace. Only about twenty more sharks, and he'd finally have enough teeth to get that awful thing around his neck.

Personally, I thought it was macabre.

Over time we've learned to like the taste of algae. Algae blooms can be quite nutritious, and there's certainly enough of it around to keep one satiated. We've also started to consume a fair amount of sea junk. Not everything, of course. Plastic bags and bottles do no more for us than for any water creature. Nasty stuff.

But the odd twist of old rope, or a good bit of metal? They both supply some necessary roughage, and keep us satisfied enough that we aren't tempted to nibble on our friends.

Why do humans think everything wants to devour them? I can only surmise that most of them haven't eaten a person. Horrible, stringy things. Even the plump ones are mostly bone, and they stink beyond belief. I'll take blue-green algae over a million tankers filled with humans.

Because we're so massive and our metabolism has slowed to a sluggish crawl, a lot of our day is spent searching for food and grazing on algae, but what else is there to do? We don't have to worry about predators, our homes have been perfect for millennia, and our children practically raise themselves.

Humans need not fear becoming my dinner. They can fear me for other reasons, but I'll leave them for the sharks before I taste any of their flesh myself. Even my wife would rather pass. Her tastes run to the carnal more than mine do, but there are certain lows to which she will not stoop, and eating humans is one of them. Oh sure, she'd tear them apart for sport, but actually consume any? Never in a million years.

The female scientist had won my grudging respect. It was a good idea of hers, suggesting the young man fix the boat in the evening. It appeared the link between us was working both ways—she could sense when I was around and when I was not. It puzzled me that she kept discussing her plans when she knew I would be listening. Was it a trick? Why would she let me know everything the humans planned to do beforehand, if she was actually on their side? But perhaps she wasn't. I'd sensed from the very beginning that she was conflicted about the work she did. It was funny how her compatriots denigrated her, when she was the only reason they were still alive.

That and my sweet nature, of course.

I left the humans to their own devices that evening so I could go home and be with my family, as always, but I planned to return later that night. I hated to prove the woman wrong, and ostracize her even further from her friends, but my curiosity couldn't be helped. The thought of the humans guarding their toy boat with their puny weapons was a sight that could not be missed. There were few occasions for comedy in this world.

Perhaps I'd let them fix their boat after all. Their entertainment value was waning, and their bickering and infighting was getting on my nerves. The ocean was supposed to be a peaceful place, and anyone who didn't understand that shouldn't be there.

It would be best if the humans repaired that joke of a vessel and went back to where they came from. It'd be quiet again. My wife would be happy, and returning to my life of tedium would be somewhat of a relief.

Once they leave our territory, I can only hope they don't return.

CHAPTER EIGHTEEN

Black above and black below.

When the water hit Thor's legs, he had second thoughts. The ocean was cold, much colder than during the day, and he could feel its chill through the wetsuit.

"One hard tug on the line, and we'll have you back here," Apostolos promised, his face a white blur above. Thor gave him a thumbs-up.

Flora motioned for the captain to keep his voice down. Her plan would only work if everyone were quiet. Too much noise, she warned, might summon the creature. The thought was enough to make Thor's balls shrivel. More than once that day he wished he'd gone for a cushy office job. What was so great about adventure, anyway? Adventure got you killed.

Liam's face floated in front of Thor as he was lowered into the water. The young engineer looked sad and worried, but there was no time to question the meaning of his presence, or even to wonder if he was real. In another second, Thor was submerged. He tightened his grip on the harpoon gun. His tools were strapped around his waist.

He'd worried that the dive lights weren't going to be enough, but they worked like a charm. It didn't take him more than a second or two to see the problem.

"Good Christ," he said, nearly dislodging his breathing tube.

The cable that connected the propellers to the engine was in bad shape. One of the propellers was crumpled like the petals of a day-old flower, and both were coated in fouling. That would have been bad enough, but it wasn't the worst of it.

There was a jagged tear under the engine room that was taking in water. Not enough to be visible from inside yet, but it wouldn't be long. God knows how much damage the leak had already done. Salt water was highly corrosive.

The tear would have to be welded, the cable repaired. This definitely wasn't going to be a one-trip job.

Selecting the tools he needed, Thor got to work detaching the damaged access panel underneath the engine room. It was a difficult task. The nuts were tight, already coated with hardened sea gunk. Swearing under his breath, he wondered when the barge had last been properly cleaned.

Don't call her a barge; she's sensitive.

Thor had the first nut secured in his tool belt before he felt it. It was the strangest sensation one could have in the ocean—the feeling of being watched. He'd only felt that one other time underwater. In that case, a tiger shark had been stalking him. If he hadn't found an old wreck to squeeze into, he probably wouldn't have survived.

When Thor turned his head, the vast darkness before him brightened, but only for a few feet. He couldn't see anything ahead, but he could feel it. And the feeling was getting stronger.

Fuck.

His fingers were numb as he worked the wrench, torqueing his wrist in order to get the nuts loosened as quickly as possible.

Why did I listen to Flora? The guys were right. I've been thinking with my—

Something swam past him. Something *big*.

Its wake slammed him into the boat, his helmet hitting metal with a clang that reverberated through his brain.

Fuck. Fuck, fuck, fuck.

Sacrificing himself for the rest of the crew wasn't noble any longer. In fact, it was pretty fucking idiotic. He was the youngest. The other guys had already had full lives. Why wasn't one of them down here risking his ass? Because they weren't young enough to be that naïve, that's why.

There was an uncomfortable pressure on his lungs. Without noticing, he'd started to hyperventilate—never a good thing when one was dependent on a breathing tube. He checked over his shoulder and shone a light into the darkness. Nothing but a few silvery fish, but whatever he was sensing hadn't gone anywhere.

It was waiting, watching.

What happened if it came closer the next time?

The line that tethered him to the ship jerked around his waist, making him gasp. Thor recognized the signal—Apostolos had seen something and wanted to bring him in. But he couldn't let this be a wasted trip. Who knew when or if he'd have the guts to return?

He frantically worked the last few nuts, ignoring the now-incessant tugging and the strong feeling of foreboding. When the last nut was off, he answered the signal with one of his own. He was yanked out of the water so fast he nearly lost his grip on the line.

"Slow down," he yelled as his body crashed into the ship. "You're going too fast."

But his voice was no match for Flora's. Now that he was above the surface, he could hear her screaming.

"Get him out of there. It's coming!"

That was all he needed to hear. Thor cycled his legs in a mad scramble-climb, much as Liam had. He saw the sad, wounded face of the engineer in front of him again, and recognized it for what it had been—a warning.

Apostolos was using every ounce of strength to bring Thor in, but it wasn't enough. Thor couldn't see where the creature was, but he could tell from the intensity of Flora's screams that it wasn't far away.

The ship lurched like a drunken sailor, throwing him to the side and almost off the rope.

Apostolos cursed. "Shit. George, come over here. I need your help."

For a second, George's big head appeared over the side of the ship. But before Thor had a chance to feel a moment of relief, the man was gone. Apostolos's muscles strained as he fought to bring Thor the rest of the way in.

"What are you babbling about? Good God, man, I need your help. We're going to lose him."

Thor froze on the line when he heard the desperation in the captain's voice.

This is it. I'm dead. This is how it ends.

It wasn't George but Frank who added his strength to Apostolos's. In just a few seconds, Thor lay gasping on the deck. Ripping the breathing tube from his mouth, he panted like a dying dog. He stared at George through bleary eyes.

The big man scowled in return, his massive arms folded across his chest.

Apostolos charged toward him until they were standing nose to nose, but George didn't so much as blink.

"What in the hell was that? If we'd lost Anderssen, it would have been on your head, you bloody coward."

"Ain't no coward," George said, his eyes narrowing until they were slits. Thor feared for the safety of his boss. "I told you from the beginning I didn't want no part of this."

"You lost that option when you signed on as part of this crew, George. We have to work together if there's going to be any chance of going home. You want to go home, don't you?"

Adrenaline was coursing through Thor's body, rendering him weak and light-headed. He managed to push himself into a sitting position to keep an eye on the two men. Apostolos sounded surprisingly reasonable. Thor didn't trust it.

Reasonable or not, the Greek's pleas weren't having the slightest effect on George, who continued to glare at Apostolos.

"He thinks you mean to sacrifice him," Flora volunteered, earning her an ugly look from George.

"I can speak for myself. I don't need you putting words in my mouth," George said. As her face flushed and she lowered her eyes, Thor wished he had the breath to give that man a piece of his mind. There was no call to treat Flora like that.

"That's preposterous, Washington. You can't seriously believe that. We need every single man we have left. Why would you—?"

George interrupted Apostolos with so much ferocity that the big Greek retreated a step. "You wanted to use me as bait to protect your sweet white boy's ass," he said, stabbing the captain's chest with one of his thick fingers. "Don't think I don't know it. As soon as you think Anderssen's in trouble, what do you try to do? Offer me as bait. I'm not that dumb."

"He asked for your help, George. No one was trying to use you for bait." Thor raised his voice to be heard over their arguing, but George ignored him. The big man's chest heaved with every breath and his nostrils flared. Unless someone figured out how to calm him down, Apostolos could very well be a dead man.

"Sorry to interrupt, but we really have to get out of here. It's not safe to be on deck right now." Thor watched in horror as Flora stretched a tentative hand toward George's arm. It was too late to warn her.

As soon as her nails grazed his shirt, the big man reacted, pushing her into the side of the ship with such force that she fell on her ass, stunned.

"Don't touch me, witch. I don't want any of your bad luck rubbing off on me."

It was over in a second.

Before Apostolos could admonish George, or help Flora.

Before anyone could breathe.

A tremendous roar split the air like a sonic boom. Thor clutched his head, pushing his hands tight to his ears as tears ran down his cheeks. Frank and Archie were writhing in pain as well. Thor noticed a vein of blood oozing between Archie's fingers. It looked black in the dim light.

Apostolos dropped to his knees, his mouth stretched in a scream no one could hear. Curling her knees to her chest, Flora huddled against the side of the boat.

The only one who didn't react to the sound was George, and that's because George wasn't there anymore.

His body had been sheared from below the waist, leaving his torso and head behind. As he flopped around the deck like a fish in an expanding pool of his own fluids, Thor stared at the thick gray ropes protruding from him until he realized what they were.

He leaned over and threw up.

* * *

Frank was the first to recover. He yelled George's name, and would have gotten to the man if Apostolos hadn't shoved him away hard enough to make him stagger.

"Don't touch him," the Greek bellowed, and his eyes were lifeless in the dying light. Thor saw no feeling in them—nothing human.

"Captain, we have to help him. He's going to die if I don't put pressure on that wound."

None of us said what we were thinking—that George was already dead, even as he gasped and writhed on the deck.

Apostolos shoved Frank again, more roughly this time. "Do you want to die too? Have you forgotten what happened to Liam?"

Frank's mouth worked as he fought to regain control of his emotions. "We can't just leave him there. He's suffering."

"Tomkins, put on some gloves. I want you to toss him overboard," Apostolos said to Archie, who couldn't have looked more stunned if the big Greek had slapped him. "Now—move your ass. We don't have much time before that shit starts eating through the planks. It's probably happening already."

Archie and Frank exchanged uneasy glances. The grunting noises from George were so awful Thor wanted to keep his hands over his ears. But now would be a bad time not to know what was happening. Flora stared at him, stricken. He motioned to her to stay put.

"Move your ass," Apostolos said at full volume, making everyone flinch. Everyone but Frank, who was glowering at the captain much as George had moments before.

"I'm not going to do that, Captain. It's murder." Archie straightened his shoulders. No one had seen Archie stand up to anyone before, let alone the Greek, and Thor sure as shit didn't want to see it now.

"Have you both lost your minds? Are you out of your fucking heads? He's already dead. You're prolonging his suffering by standing there like fools."

A terrible gurgling came from George. Thor prayed for it to be over soon.

"The longer he lies on that deck, the more of that acid—or whatever it is—eats into the ship. Is that what you want? For everyone else to die, just so a doomed man can live out his last moments in extreme pain?"

When Archie and Frank refused to move, Apostolos lost it. He stormed across the deck and grabbed a pair of gloves, snapping the heavy black rubber over his wrists and forearms.

"Fucking useless bits of pussy," the Greek growled. "There isn't one of you on this ship that's worth a goddamn thing."

He seized George under the arms, careful to avoid the man's gaping wound. Incredibly, George's hands clutched at Apostolos's sleeves. He shook his head while Flora sobbed and turned away.

But Apostolos didn't hesitate. He hefted George's body over the side like it was an anchor. Thor flinched at the resounding splash, longing to retreat into the oblivion of unconsciousness, but unwilling to leave Apostolos alone. It didn't take a genius to see the captain was in danger.

Archie and Frank ran at him, but the big Greek rallied before they could touch him.

"What are you thinking? Going to throw me overboard maybe?" Apostolos spat on the deck at their feet. "I'd like to see you sail this fucking boat without me."

"There are good sailors on this boat, Apostolos." Frank sneered at him. "We don't need you."

"I just saved your worthless lives, you idiots." The Greek hollered in their faces, but the men were unmoved. Grasping the side of the ship, Thor pulled himself upright. There was no way he could defend Apostolos from both Frank and Archie, but maybe together they could pose enough of a challenge to convince the men to back off.

As Thor took a few staggering steps, he realized his plan was laughable. He'd been hired for his brains, not his brawn. Frank could send him flying with one hand tied behind his back. The best he could do was use his intellect to reason with them, and they didn't seem like they were in a reasonable mood.

"Look."

It was Flora who stopped the mutiny before it began as the men turned to see what she was pointing at. George's blood bubbled on the deck. Once everyone quit yelling for a minute, they heard the sound—a noxious sizzling that reminded Thor of Liam's death. His stomach churned, and he staggered to the side of the ship to vomit.

"It's dissolving the wood." Flora's voice had a hysterical edge, and her words were enough to spur the men into action. Buckets of seawater cleansed the deck, washing the last of George over the side.

When it was done, the five-member crew stood panting. Sweat trickled down Thor's neck under the stifling wetsuit.

"We need to get down below," Flora said, and this time, everyone listened to her. "It isn't safe here."

But before they could make it to the stairs, Apostolos raised his hand. "Wait. A moment of respect for Washington."

Feeling the tears burn his eyes, Thor lowered his head. He'd never be able to erase the image of the big man's terrible death from his mind. Archie took off his cap.

"They that go down to the sea in ships, and occupy their business on the great waters; these men see the works of the Lord, and his wonders in the deep. For at his word, the stormy wind ariseth, which lifteth the waves thereof," Apostolos said. Flora leaned against Thor's shoulder, and he could feel her body shaking. Wrapping his arm around her, he pulled her close, seeking a comfort he feared he would never find.

"They are carried to the heaven, and down again to the deep— their soul melteth away because of the trouble. They reel to and fro, and stagger like a drunken man, and are at their wits' end. So they cry unto the Lord in their trouble, and he delivereth them from their distress.

"For he maketh the storm to cease, so that the waves thereof are still. Then are they glad, because they are at rest; and so he bringeth them unto the haven where they would be. Amen."

"Amen," Thor whispered.

CHAPTER NINETEEN

It was Frank who first mentioned it.

Flora never ceased to be amazed by the way men handled conflict. A short hour before, Frank and Archie had been prepared to throw Apostolos to his death, and now they acted as if an ugly word had never been exchanged. To his credit, Apostolos was going along with it. If their captain held a grudge, he was hiding it well.

"What are we going to do, Captain?" Archie asked.

"Obviously we can't risk sleeping above deck anymore. We'll have to avoid going topside as much as possible. It isn't safe." The big Greek ran a hand over his weary face, as exhausted as she'd ever seen him.

The chorus of groans and protests she'd expected never came.

Frank turned blurry eyes on her. "I thought it was safe at night. I thought the monster was at home, or in its lair, or wherever the fuck it sleeps. Isn't that what you told us?"

Fear and guilt made her stiffen, but Apostolos responded before she could. "Let's not start with that again. Duchovney is flying blind, same as the rest of us. None of us know what that creature is, so how in the hell can we predict how it'll react?"

"She's still responsible for another man's death," Frank muttered, and Flora clenched her bottle of beer, wondering if she'd be forced to use it as a weapon. If Frank attacked her, she'd go down fighting.

"She's no more responsible than I am. Blame me if you need someone to pin this on. I'm the one who sent Anderssen to fix the ship, and I'm the one who called George for help. Duchovney had nothing to do with it."

From the stubborn expression on his face, Frank clearly thought otherwise, but thankfully he kept his mouth shut. Flora wasn't sure how much longer she could listen to his misogynistic bullshit.

"Did anyone actually *see* a creature?" Archie asked. "I was too busy trying to protect my ears. And then suddenly George was...you know. I didn't really get a look at the thing."

Flora took a deep breath. "I did."

Frank snorted. "Of course *you* did."

"I've about had it with you, Hearne. Duchovney is a part of this crew, just like anyone else. You need to start paying her some respect," Apostolos warned. His thick black brows came together in a frown that, for once, was not meant for her.

"But can't you see what she's doing? She'll say anything to support her original theory," Frank said, keeping his face averted as he gestured in her direction. "Of course she's going to say she saw a creature. I want to hear from someone *else* who saw it."

"I saw it too, Frank."

Frank's head swiveled in surprise until he saw the speaker was Thor. He made a big show of smacking his forehead. "Oh, that's a shocker. Now the scientist's little lover has seen it. Anyone else who *isn't* completely biased?"

"Everyone felt something. And we definitely all heard something," Apostolos said, indicating the trail of blood that had dried on his neck. Out of everyone on the crew, only Flora's ears hadn't bled. She wasn't sure why, as the sound had been as painful for her as it had been for everyone else. "I don't need to lay eyes on this thing myself in order to believe them. If there's no creature, what do you think happened to George? Or do you think I hacked him in half when no one was looking?"

Flora's chest tightened at the thought of the man's mutilated body fighting to save itself. It was a horror she'd never be able to forget.

"I don't know what to think," Frank said. But the anger was gone from his voice.

Apostolos sighed. "None of us do. These creatures are the stuff of mythology. No one really believes they exist." He focused on Flora, his eyes red-rimmed and unbearably sad. She realized how much the big man cared about his crew. "How would you describe it, Flora?"

She started when Apostolos used her given name, but recovered quickly. She wanted to talk about it—*needed* to talk about it. For the first time in a long while, she yearned for her scientific colleagues. "It had a long neck, almost like a snake's. When it reared over the boat, it reminded me of a cobra. It had a narrow, flat head with a wide mouth—lots of sharp teeth." She shuddered, remembering. Thankfully, she'd looked away before the creature bit George, but she'd still seen enough to give her nightmares for the rest of her life. "It—it sounds silly, but it resembled a dinosaur. What kind of dinosaur, I don't know, but it was gigantic. We can't possibly fight it."

When she met Thor's eyes across the table and he tilted his head at her in a slight nod, she sagged with relief. Her credibility had taken a beating in the past week, and the last thing she wanted was more accusations.

Their silent exchange didn't go unnoticed. "Is that what you saw too, Anderssen?" Apostolos asked.

"Yeah, except it was bigger than any fossil I've ever seen. Its neck was so long and massive I didn't get to see the rest of its body. It was a grayish-green, or at least that's what it appeared like to me."

"Why would it attack George?" Frank said. "He was just standing on deck. He should have been safe from that thing."

Flora bit her lip. "I do have a theory, but it's going to sound crazy."

"Go ahead, Duchovney. I think we're past the point of disbelief now," Apostolos said.

"Well, these animals—whatever they are—appear to be fairly sensitive. I'm not sure how to explain how I know this—I just do." Her voice sounded stronger than she felt. *Maybe I'm finally getting some confidence again.* Glancing around the table, she was relieved to see that even Archie and Frank were listening. "George was upset right before it happened, and all that yelling and fighting—I think it might have caused the creature to attack."

"You're saying George is to blame? Woman, have you no heart? Did you not see what happened to him?" Frank's face flushed with anger, but she didn't hold his reaction against him. Two members of their crew were gone, and there weren't many left.

"Of course I did. But I think we should learn from this. I don't know about you, but I'm not keen to see anyone else die."

"What's that supposed to mean? That I—"

Apostolos cleared his throat. "That's enough. Duchovney's right. We need to start working together, if for no other reason than this sniping and bickering is making my head hurt."

"How can we possibly work together when we don't trust her?" Frank pointed at Flora, who gritted her teeth in fury.

Apostolos pounded his fist on the table. "I said *enough*. We've had a rocky go of it, and I admit I haven't helped. I was right pissed when the drill was destroyed, and I took it out on Duchovney. But we need to move past that. Lashay is dead. Washington is dead. And for whatever reason, Duchovney is the only one here who has some insight into why that creature reacts the way it does."

"How do we know she's not the reason the creature is here in the first place? Maybe she *summoned* it."

If the situation hadn't been so horrible, Flora would have laughed. "You can't seriously think I can summon it. If I had that kind of power, I would have sent it away a long time ago."

Frank glared at her. "For all we know, you want this ship for yourself, and you won't be happy until the rest of us are dead."

She slumped in her seat, clutching at her dark curls with both hands. If she couldn't smack some sense into Frank, maybe she'd tear her own hair out instead. "All I want is to go home to my son. That's it. I just want to go home."

Her voice cracked on the word *home*, and she hid her face behind her curtain of hair.

Someone patted her hand, and she was shocked to see it was Archie. He gave her a weak smile, really nothing more than a slight twitch of the lips. "I believe you, Flora. I don't think you had anything to do with any of it."

"Thank you," she whispered.

"Of *course* she didn't have anything to do with it," Thor said, the exasperation audible in his voice. "Frank, what are you thinking? You haven't been making any sense since Liam died."

The sailor's chair screeched across the wood planking as he pushed himself away from the table. Without another word, he left the group.

"I hope he doesn't go on deck," Archie said.

"Wherever he goes, he needs to cool off. His temper is getting out of control." Thor unclenched his fists, and Flora guessed she wasn't the only one who'd wanted to hit the older man. "What's his problem, anyway?"

Archie stared at his hands while he played with a butter knife left behind from lunch. "I think he blames himself for what happened to Liam. He was the one who was going to take care of the kid, and he stitched that leg. He told me afterward that he doesn't understand why he didn't notice anything was wrong. He thought the wound looked normal."

"Did he cut the man's leg? Did he pour that ghastly acid into him? What happened to Lashay is no one's fault—at least no one on this ship." Apostolos rose from the table. "I'll go talk to him."

"I wouldn't, boss. Sometimes Frank needs to work things out for himself," Archie said, rubbing a calloused thumb along the side of his nose. "I can tell when he wants to be left alone."

They sat in silence for a few minutes, their thoughts weighing heavily on their minds. Flora's eyelids drooped, but she wasn't in a hurry to return to her cabin alone. What if the creature decided to destroy the ship while they slept? She had a good idea how big it was now, and it was certainly possible. It was capable of tearing apart a vessel ten times the size of *The Cormorant*.

"So what's next?" Archie asked, startling her awake. "We can't sit here waiting until that thing gets hungry again."

They waited for Apostolos's command, but for once, the captain didn't appear to have the answer. The Greek swiped sweat from his forehead with one of his thick-fingered hands, staring at the worn wooden table as if hoping it would tell him what to do. "Anderssen, can you get to work on that radio? See if you can fix it. We need to send out a distress signal."

Thor nodded, but before he could say anything, Flora spoke up. "Are you sure it's such a good idea to bring others out here?"

"I don't see as how we have any choice. Our supplies won't last forever. The ship ain't running. We may need to be towed in." As Apostolos assessed her, she had the uneasy feeling he could read her mind. She suspected the Greek was more intelligent than she'd given him credit for. "What are you thinking, Duchovney?"

Flora tucked her hands under her arms to warm them. "Everything was fine until we sent the drill down. That's what triggered this. I did the surveys myself, and there was *nothing* down there. The area was clear."

"There wasn't anything on sonar," Thor said.

"But our drill was destroyed—by something with large teeth. And then Liam was attacked—"

"Skip the recap. What's your point?" Apostolos said.

"I think the creature is territorial. It's attacking because we're on its turf, and that's why it destroyed the drill as well. It doesn't want us here."

A deep laugh rumbled from Apostolos's chest, but there was little humor in it. "That's been established."

"If I'm right and the creature *is* territorial, bringing another ship into the area would be a disaster. We'd be sending the next crew to their deaths, not to mention putting ourselves in more jeopardy."

"We have to try something. Tomkins is right—we can't sit and wait until that monster is hungry again. I'm responsible for the lives of this crew." Apostolos pointed at Thor. "I promised your mother I'd get you home in one piece, and I'm a man of my word."

Thor reddened at the mention of his mother. "I can fix the cable, Captain. It's been mangled to shit, but I know I can do it."

"And then what? Are you going to hold it over your head while you spin around and fly us away from here? There's no bloody way I'm letting you get into that water again."

"I still think it can be done, if we keep our shit together and stay quiet. Flora has a point. Nothing attacked while I was down there. The creature didn't strike until the fighting broke out on deck. And George was yelling the loudest."

Apostolos shook his head. "I won't hear any more about it. My decision on this is final, Anderssen. You're too valuable. Now that Lashay is gone, you're our only engineer. We'd die without you."

"You'll die with me too. You know there's a good chance we're not going to get out of this, Apostolos. At least let me try."

The big Greek rubbed his bristly chin and gave what was left of his crew a pained look. "Augh. I need some time to think. I have to plan a strategy." He stood, his chair creaking alarmingly. "I'm turning in. I'll see you in the morning."

The remaining three said their goodnights. Flora waited until Apostolos was out of earshot before she spoke. "He's right, you know. I can't believe you would even suggest it."

"What other choice do we have? We have to do something, and I know I can fix the engine. Once the cable's been repaired, it'll take me fifteen minutes, tops."

"Did you see what happened to George? How long do you think that took?" *Why are men so dumb? Why are they always so damn willing to die?*

Archie gave her a sympathetic smile. "Sometimes a man needs to take a risk. Often the risks are foolish, yes, but without them, life wouldn't be worth living."

"This is not an extreme sport. This is a creature that's hell-bent on killing us. If you're going to take a risk, at least make it a calculated one. What you're talking about is suicide, and that's not going to help anyone on this ship."

Both men stared at her, silenced. She forced herself to meet their eyes without blinking. Someone had to speak the truth. Someone had to point out that stubbornness was one of the reasons they'd gotten into this mess. If Liam hadn't been so headstrong, so determined to take photos of the creature, he'd still be alive.

"Okay, Flora. What's your suggestion? What do you think we should do?"

At Thor's question, the fatigue of the past few days hit her.

"Can I tell you in the morning? I'm too tired to think right now."

* * *

The two men insisted on walking her to her cabin, even though it was across the hall. She was touched by their kindness. George's death had been terrible, but with his absence, the mood on the ship had lightened considerably. Now that Apostolos was on her side, there was no reason for her to feel threatened anymore.

And yet she did.

CHAPTER TWENTY

My wife spent the next twenty minutes gargling salt water.

Draugen always did have a flair for the dramatic.

"Blech." She spat, expelling a great gob of ichor that sizzled on the rock walls. "I forgot how *juicy* they are. Disgusting." She peered at me, expecting sympathy most likely, and I quickly moved my head to hide the reprobation in my eyes.

Too late.

"Don't you dare look at me that way, Nøkken. You know I could snap your neck in a second flat."

Keeping my head averted, I attempted to swim past her. The night had been ruined. I figured I might as well make the best of it and sleep for a few hours, but she cut me off, blocking my path.

"You're sulking. Actually sulking, like a child. I swear, between you and our son, sometimes I don't know which needs raising."

"If you are ever in doubt, I can clarify it for you, *dearheart*." I forced the endearment from between clenched teeth, which had the desired affect—my wife paused. She rarely saw anger from me, so when she did, she usually respected it. At least, I *hope* she respected it. I'd always assumed that's the only reason I'm still here.

"This isn't about the humans, is it? Whatever is this obsession with them? I've never known you to be so single-minded."

I lunged at her, roaring in her face.

"We discussed this. We *agreed*. There was to be no killing of humans. Thanks to you, they're going to have the entire Navy here within a few days."

"That's a bit like the sky calling the ocean blue, isn't it, Nøkken? I recall you killed the first one."

I swallowed hard, trying not to picture what had happened to the young engineer. It hadn't been my fault, but I'd been nauseous with guilt ever since. "That was an accident. What you did tonight was murder."

She snorted, and the resulting wake pushed me back a foot. "Murder? No more than eating a shark, and we've done plenty of that. Since when do we care about the survival of such miserable, destructive creatures?"

Deciding to use the only tactic that might stand a chance of working, I appealed to her ego. "Slaughtering innocents is something they would do. We're superior to them, remember? We've evolved past them, and yet tonight you acted exactly like they'd expect—like a monster."

Draugen pushed past me, slamming me into the rock wall so my ears rang. "This is ridiculous. I'm going to bed. I'm sorry to have embarrassed you in front of your wee friends, Nøkken."

"You don't understand, do you? They *saw* you. They know what you look like now. Forget the Navy—they'll have CNN on our backsides before we can blink. Remember Uisge? We'll have to move."

My wife's expression changed. We'd been on the verge of a battle that would have left our son without a father, but now she looked almost pleased. Happy, even. I didn't have to ask why.

"Are you suggesting I kill all of them, darling?"

"No, of course not. You shouldn't have killed one."

"No human is going to force me out of my home. If Uisge had simply eaten a bunch of them a long time ago, like I told her, she wouldn't have the problems she has today."

"We can't wipe out the species, Draugen. There are too many."

"No, not the entire species. Just the ones who venture into the ocean."

I pictured the bloodshed that would result if our kind engaged the humans in open war. There was no doubt we would prevail, but at too great a cost. The humans would use every weapon at their disposal, poisoning the oceans and slaughtering billions of smaller sea creatures without compunction. If they murdered their own kind without a quiver of conscience, they certainly wouldn't trouble themselves over the suffering of dolphins or whales. Or the poor beleaguered shark.

Still, it used to be a fantasy of mine, I'll admit. Each time the sludge of yet another oil spill reached us—every time I had to bite through one of their miserable nets to rescue a dolphin pod—I dreamed of crunching human skulls between my teeth. I didn't blame my wife for being puzzled by my recent reversal; I was confused myself. These humans had come into our territory for the sole purpose of polluting our home, and for that, they deserved to die. Another time I would have slaughtered them alongside my wife, relishing the crew's screams of pain before I silenced them forever.

I wasn't sure why this particular ship was different. There was a female—that was new, but it wasn't like I had some strange affinity for the women of their species. I had enough trouble with the women in my own.

We'd had previous experience with what humans called 'engineers,' and to a one, they'd been dull, tedious men who used their brains for profit instead of the greater good. We detest short-term thinking.

The same shortsightedness didn't appear to be present on this particular ship, at least not in the female or the unfortunate young man I'd nicked with my tail.

But after the engineer died, something had changed. I could feel it, and my wife could as well. She was extremely sensitive to conflict—always had been—but that wasn't the only thing she had reacted to. I knew the arguing wasn't the only reason she'd killed tonight.

Perhaps I was getting more fanciful as I neared middle age, but a dark cloud hovered over that ship. I'd seen this before, and it never ended well. Call me sentimental, but I didn't want the woman stuck on a ghost ship, sailing through eternity with a crew of damned souls. I wanted her to escape and return to her son—for some reason, she felt a desperate love for that boy. It intrigued me, simply because I could not muster it for my own.

In any case, I didn't presume she'd return to the oil business anytime soon. If my original intent had been to issue a warning, that warning had been received. You might say my work here was done. Now I just needed to leave the humans to their own devices—let them prepare their little boat.

Unfortunately, I couldn't promise my wife would do the same.

CHAPTER TWENTY-ONE

The hand slammed over her mouth, grinding her lips into her teeth. Flora's eyes flew open, widening when she saw the angry face leaning over her. She fought to breathe, forcing air through her nose and struggling to pull away, but she couldn't move. The man's body pinned her to her bunk.

If she'd had any doubt as to his intent, it was gone as soon as he spoke.

"Stuck-up bitch," he hissed at her, spittle striking her face. "You think you're too good for me, don't you? You think you're too good for the whole bloody lot of us."

She tried to shake her head, but his hand held her fast. Along with the blood from her injured lip, she could taste bitter grime and the salt of sweat from his palm. Flora remembered how dirty Frank's hands were, as if he never troubled to wash them. Her stomach churned.

The man was nose to nose with her, his eyes blazing with hate. As she fought to free herself, a dreadful sound split the night air—Frank's zipper. She pushed against him even harder.

"I want to see how good you are. It's been a long time since I've had a woman who wasn't a twenty-dollar whore. Let's see if someone as high-minded as you can teach me a thing or two. Why should you save it for the boy when you can have a man?"

Flora's mind reeled with the moves from every self-defense course she'd ever taken. She'd always promised herself that she'd die before she'd allow herself to be raped. But now that she was in the situation, death was the last thing she wanted.

Frank shifted his weight as he attempted to pull his jeans down while keeping his other hand clamped over her mouth. It was a small movement, but just enough that she was able to get one of her legs free. She brought her knee into the sailor's groin with all her strength, envisioning his testicles coming out his eyeballs.

"You bloody cunt." He slammed his fist into her face before she knew what was happening. She felt a strange *pop*, and the top of the other bunk swirled in front of her, interrupted by tiny starbursts that exploded in front of her eyes. Her head throbbed, and she felt something warm and wet run down the side of her face.

It wasn't what she'd expected. Frank hadn't rolled off her, incapacitated and groaning with pain. She'd only succeeded in making him angrier. But when he'd taken his hand off her mouth to punch her, he'd forgotten to put it back. Though the roaring pain in her head was enough to bring tears to her eyes, she screamed.

The door slammed open, and seconds later Frank was pulled away from her, cursing and struggling. Through swollen eyes, she watched as he took a swing at Thor before Apostolos tackled him. One punch from the Greek was all it took. Frank fell to the floor, as dead to the world as if he were in a coma.

In spite of her pain and confusion, Flora was suspicious. *How did they get here so fast?* True, Frank's yelling might have woken them before her scream, but it was almost as if the other men had been awake, waiting for something to happen. If they'd suspected she was in danger, why hadn't they warned her?

Someone bent over her and she flinched before she saw it was Thor. He reached out as if to touch her face, then drew his hand away. "Oh God, Flora. What did he do to you?"

"Is she okay?" Apostolos's accent was thicker than usual.

"No...her face is covered in blood. Can you get me a towel?"

"Bastard. Fucking monster." Flora heard a dull thud as Apostolos kicked at something on the floor, something that was most likely Frank. "I knew you were trouble from the beginning. I should have gotten rid of you a long time ago, you perverted son of a bitch."

The Greek did as Thor asked, and soon her friend was carefully pressing a towel to her injured face. The ice water oozing from the terrycloth was so cold it made her gasp.

"Shh…it's okay now."

His words made her furious. His words, and his tone. He sounded as if he were talking to a child. She'd been attacked, but she was far from a baby. She struggled to sit up, pushing his hand away.

"Flora, you need to keep this on your face. It'll bring the swelling down."

"It's not okay. How can you say that? It's a million miles from okay. That asshole tried to rape me."

And he called me a cunt. She wished there was a male equivalent she could use for him, but sadly, the filthiest curse words were always female.

"I know. Thank God we got here in time."

"I would have killed him before I'd let him rape me." Now that the threat was past, it was easy to forget how terrified she'd been, how the weight of Frank's body had prevented her from moving, let alone fighting.

"I might kill him anyway," Apostolos said, giving Frank another kick. He directed a flood of angry Greek at the man, and Flora knew they were curse words. She only hoped the Greeks had better options than the English. "I'm sorry, Duchovney. I gave you my word that you'd be safe here. I've failed you as a captain."

"It's not your fault," she said, hating the weakness she could hear in her voice as the adrenaline wore off. She could feel the pain from her injured nose now, and she meekly accepted the towel from Thor and held it to her face, grateful she couldn't see how much blood she'd lost. "You had no way of knowing he was a monster."

"I saw the anger in him. His temper was always a problem. But I never thought he'd do anything like this. I'm of a mind to throw him overboard."

"What's going on?"

The three of them turned to see Archie standing in the doorway. His eyes flicked from Frank, who was still dead to the world, over to Flora, who was using every bit of resolve she had to keep from weeping. Her hand trembled madly as she tried to keep pressure on her injured nose, but she wouldn't let Thor help. Even though she knew the attack was no one's fault but Frank's, she couldn't afford to let them see her as a victim. She didn't have the luxury of being anyone's damsel in distress.

"Did you know anything about this, Tomkins?" Apostolos asked, surprising her. Archie had always been quiet and well mannered. She couldn't imagine him having any part in what Frank had tried to do to her.

"Know anything about what? I heard a lot of yelling and screaming, and I come in here and she looks like she's been in a brawl—" Archie nodded toward Flora, "and Frank is on the floor."

"He's your bunkmate," Apostolos said, his voice low and dangerous. What the captain had done to Frank hadn't been enough—Flora could see he wanted to hurt someone, and hurt them bad. She hoped Archie would tread carefully.

"Hey, I'm not my bunkmate's keeper. Frank often wanders around at night. It's gotten so it doesn't wake me anymore."

At Archie's words, Flora felt her heart stop. She thought of all the times she'd been startled awake in the middle of the night, terrified, never understanding the reason for her fear. But now she remembered a sound that had consistently invaded her dreams—a familiar sound that made her want to hide.

"Has he tried this before, Duchovney?" Apostolos sounded so ferocious she was afraid to answer, but she saw no reason to protect the monster in their midst.

"I—I think so. I didn't realize it until now, but someone's tried to get in my room before. The sound of the doorknob turning always woke me." Thor's cheeks were flushed as he mouthed a silent apology for not protecting her. She would have to tell him later that he had nothing to feel bad about. Frank had been cantankerous, and often misogynistic, but there was no warning he'd been capable of this. Even Flora, who knew her instincts were pretty good, hadn't thought the man was dangerous. "I've always locked my door, but tonight I left it open." Her voice sounded thick and muffled, as if she had a bad cold. In spite of Thor's care, her nose was swelling, making it difficult to breathe. "I thought it would be safer."

She could see the shock in Archie's eyes as the truth dawned on him. "*Frank* did that to you? But why?"

"Because he's a sorry excuse for a human being, that's why," Thor said.

"I'm just glad you guys got here when you did. I thought I could fight my way out of anything, but nothing worked. I even kneed him in the balls, but all it did was make him angry. That's when he hit me."

The men groaned in unison, startling her. Even Archie was shaking his head.

"What? What did I say? I had to defend myself."

"It's not that," Thor said. "It's just—well, movies and TV and even those self-defense courses give women the wrong impression. They tell you that if you're ever attacked, you only need to knee the guy in the balls, and he'll drop like a stone."

Her brain swam with confusion. That *was* what she'd been taught. "What's wrong with that?"

"It's not true. Well, maybe once in a blue moon it's true, but I wouldn't count on it. For one thing, it's not as easy to hit them square on as women think, and if you graze them, it won't tickle, but it's not going to incapacitate us, either."

"Go for the eyes, Duchovney," Apostolos said. "Always go for the eyes. Jab your fingers at them, hard as you can."

"Or the throat. If you have the leeway, hit the guy here." Thor pantomimed a punch to Archie's Adam's apple. "If you hit hard enough, you can kill someone. Game over."

Flora's stomach fluttered with nausea, and she closed her eyes. "I appreciate the pointers, but I hope this was a one-time thing."

"Which brings us to the issue at hand. What are we going to do about Frank? Obviously we can't have him roaming the ship," Thor said.

She heard the dull thud of Apostolos kicking Frank's body. "I still say we donate him to our monster friend. Maybe he'd like some well-aged meat for a change."

"I'm really sorry, Flora."

She opened her eyes to see Archie watching her anxiously, his round face pale and solemn.

"I had no idea where he was going. I thought he was taking a walk on deck," he said. "The few nights I was awake when he left, he told me he was getting some air. If I'd known—"

"It wasn't your fault, Archie. Nobody knew."

"I should have, though. Bloody pathetic excuse for a man." Apostolos kicked Frank again, and this time the sailor groaned in response. "Yeah, wake up, you bastard. Wake up so I can pop you again."

"Why don't we tie him up and put him in the cargo hold?" Archie said. "He can stay there until we get to shore. He won't be able to hurt anybody down there."

The big Greek shook his head. "I still like the idea of throwing him overboard."

CHAPTER TWENTY-TWO

If Thor had learned anything, it was that you should never believe things couldn't get any worse.

They always could.

Once Frank came to and realized he was trussed in the cargo hold, he was angrier than a junkyard dog. He hollered and cursed for the rest of the night, and then through the next day, and Flora was right about the creature not liking discord. It bumped against the ship so hard Thor was afraid it was going to tear it apart. The poor *Cormorant* couldn't take much more abuse.

Apostolos was terrified Frank was going to get everyone killed, and when it became apparent the sailor had no intention of stopping, he ordered Thor and Archie to gag him. But they couldn't do it. Thor was a mechanical engineer and Archie a simple sailor. Neither of them was cut out for that kind of work.

Once the Greek saw they weren't going to budge, he went below and did it himself. The men heard some shouting for a while, and then nothing but muffled grunts. Frank's cries sounded like the half-hearted barking of a dying dog that didn't have much left in him.

Flora stayed in the messdeck most of the time. Thor guessed it was probably the only place she felt safe. As he popped in to check on her, he was sad to see her flinch, and enraged at Frank for destroying her spirit.

"How are you feeling?"

To be honest, she was pretty hard to look at. Seeing her face made him want to kill Frank. Her eyes were ringed with purple, her nose a swollen, angry lump. He'd done the best he could to set it, but unless a doctor broke it again once she got to shore, it would always be a little crooked. He'd told her it made her look tough, and that had at least gotten her to smile. She smiled so rarely these days.

Her lip was split, and she'd complained of a headache ever since the attack. The men had raided Frank's stash of painkillers, the irony not lost on them, but the aspirin they'd been able to find hadn't done much good.

"Won't he stop? He's driving me crazy."

"Not unless we let him out. He's a stubborn old fucker."

"Then maybe Apostolos should let him go. I don't know how much more of this I can take."

Her words shocked him. Pulling out a chair, he was careful not to scrape it against the floor. The slightest sound was enough to make Flora wince—no wonder Frank's constant barking was driving her to madness. "We can't risk him attacking you again."

"One of you could stay with me, just in case. If someone else was in the room, I don't think he would try anything."

He shook his head. "After what happened, I don't think the Greek trusts anyone that much. And how about you? Would you feel safe, knowing he was out? That he could be anywhere on board?"

Flora sighed, resting her head on her arms. "Probably not, but there has to be an alternative. This is awful."

Even Thor's noise-cancelling headphones hadn't helped her. He'd managed to get the generator working, and those with MP3 players had been able to charge them, but with Flora's constant headaches, listening to music hurt just as much.

"Maybe we should throw him overboard." He'd wanted to make her smile again, but as soon as the words were out of his mouth, he regretted it. She regarded him as if he were something slimy creeping out from under a rock.

"Don't even joke about that. As horrible as Frank is, I wouldn't wish that on anyone." Flora shuddered, and then winced. "Have you forgotten what happened to Liam?"

Of course he hadn't, though not for lack of trying. Thor figured the sight of Liam's flesh dissolving would haunt him for the rest of his life. "I'm sorry. That was my clumsy attempt to lighten the mood."

When she met his eyes, he was shocked at how sad she looked. Her eyes were those of a drowning woman, someone resigned to her death. "Maybe some moods shouldn't be lightened. Liam is gone. George is gone. I'm hurt, and Frank is confined to the hold like an animal." She sighed again. "I'm not ready to laugh about this yet, and to be honest, I'm not sure I ever will be."

"It was in poor taste. I was just—"

Apostolos interrupted his apology. It was one of the few times Thor was happy to see him.

"You're up, Anderssen."

"Huh?"

You're up was a common refrain when there was work to do, but since the ship was stranded with no drill and no electronics, the Greek had been leaving the crew to their own devices.

"The beast down below needs a pee break." Apostolos rolled his eyes. "Give him a sandwich too. God knows we don't want any squawking about human rights violations when we get to shore."

When we get to shore. It was amazing the captain managed to stay so confident. He sounded like he actually believed it, but it would be at least another week before anyone missed them, and much longer for a rescue ship to arrive. And what if the creature attacked the rescuers as well?

As far as Thor could see, unless he was able to fix the cable and stop the leak, they were doomed.

It troubled him how Apostolos had taken to calling Frank 'the beast,' as if he were somehow less than human. Did he still consider throwing the sailor overboard? It wouldn't have entirely surprised him. The captain's nerves were stretched tighter than guitar strings. It wouldn't take much to push him over the edge.

As Thor went to assemble the turkey on rye, along with whatever meager excuse for vegetables they had left, Apostolos added another task to his to-do list.

"And take Tomkins with you."

"I thought he was trying to get some sleep."

"Who can sleep in this?" Point taken. Even the Greek had to raise his voice to be heard over the commotion in the hold. The gag may have muffled Frank, but it hadn't slowed him down.

"He was dead on his feet. I can handle this myself."

Apostolos gave him a look that brooked no argument. "I don't want you handling him alone, Anderssen. Do you hear me?"

"Yes, Captain." Thor was annoyed, but also grateful.

* * *

Archie wasn't in his bunk. He also wasn't in the control room, or anywhere else Thor would expect to find him. Since he was sure Archie wasn't in the hold keeping Frank company, there was only one place left to search.

Dread overwhelmed him as he started up the steps leading to the deck. He hadn't been on deck since the terrible night George died. As far as he knew, none of them had.

When Thor cleared the staircase, the sea air hurried to greet him. In spite of his fears, it felt amazing. He took a moment to fill his lungs as his shoulders settled back where they belonged. The sun was warm on his face. This was what he'd hoped for when he decided to work on the rigs. Being on deck made him feel almost human again.

And best of all, it was another level removed from Frank. Thor could barely hear him bitching.

Archie hunched over the bow rail, his few strands of brown hair fluttering in the breeze. Even at this distance, Thor could see the man's old plaid shirt desperately needed a wash. It was covered with splotches of dried blood and who knows what else.

The boards creaked beneath Thor's feet as he crept toward Archie, aware with every step that they were both violating orders. The deck wasn't safe. As wonderful as the fresh air was, it wasn't worth their lives.

He could tell by the way Archie's body stiffened that the man realized he wasn't alone, but he kept staring over the water. When Archie was close enough to touch, Thor spoke.

"Hey, Archie?"

No response.

"The deck is off limits, remember? What are you doing? You want to catch hell from the Greek?"

The man muttered something then. Thor couldn't quite make it out, but he thought it might have alluded to what the captain could do with his orders and reprimands.

"He's only trying to keep our asses alive," Thor said, wondering what parallel universe he had stumbled into that would charge him with defending their temperamental boss. "You don't want to end up like George, do you?"

Archie turned, and his face looked terrible enough that Thor retreated a step. The man's eyes were bloodshot and so shadowed by lack of sleep that they resembled Flora's. His round face was sunken around the cheeks, and Thor didn't like his coloring. Archie's normally ruddy complexion had soured to a whitish green.

He shrugged. "What does it matter? We're going to die anyway. At least George doesn't have to suffer anymore."

There was something about seeing Archie in that state that made Thor want to give up. Archie had always been the crew's comic relief. The man, while maybe not the sharpest tool in the shed, was unfailingly happy and good-natured. They'd needed that.

They needed it more than ever now.

"I'm going to get us out of here."

Archie groaned. "You don't have to humor me no more. At first I wasn't ready to die, but I've made my peace with it. If that creature gets hungry again, it can have me. At least it will be an interesting death."

"There isn't going to be any more death, Archie."

Thor could see in Archie's face how young the other man thought he was, how young and how naïve. And maybe he was, but he couldn't curl in a ball and wait to die. He had to at least try to get them out of there.

But there was no point arguing with a defeated man. Actions spoke louder than words, and he knew the color would return to Archie's cheeks when *The Cormorant's* engine came to life beneath his feet, when they left the monster in their wake.

"It's time for Frank's bathroom break. And I've got his lunch." Thor indicated the sandwich-and-pickle plate. "Apostolos wants you to go with me."

To his surprise, Archie shook his head. Thor had never known him to say no to anyone before. "I can't."

"I know you don't like seeing him this way. None of us do. But we had no choice. We couldn't risk him going after Flora again—or anyone else. He's not in his right mind."

"It's not that. I'm sick, Thor." Archie hung his head as if ashamed, and it was then Thor realized some of the splotches on his filthy shirt were vomit. His own stomach roiled in sympathy. "I can't leave the deck. I know you probably thought I was out here because of a death wish, but the truth is, if I try to go anywhere else..." He didn't have to say another word. Thor got the picture. Sometimes being on deck in the fresh air was the only cure for seasickness.

He didn't know what to do. Frank's sandwich was getting soggier by the second, and standing in the salt spray wasn't helping matters. But Apostolos would kill him if he found out Thor had disobeyed orders.

"It'll be okay," Archie said, reading his mind. "Frank won't hurt you, and he'll be happy to have something to eat." Thor didn't miss that he kept his eyes averted from the sandwich. "He's not a monster, you know."

Thor nodded, even though he had his doubts.

* * *

The hold was pitch black and stinking. For a moment, Thor felt searing rage at the Greek—at all of them—for allowing a fellow human being to be kept in those conditions. Frank had hurt Flora, but like Archie said, he wasn't a monster. Were they any better for keeping him down there in the dark?

He was fumbling for the string to turn on the light when a harsh voice made him jump.

"Don't bother. I smashed it."

"Why?"

The question came out before he could second-guess himself. He couldn't imagine how anyone could stand it there in the foul-smelling darkness, hearing only the shuffling of the rats.

Assuming they still had rats. Perhaps the rodents were smart enough to have fled a long time ago.

"Did you know they keep the lights on in solitary confinement? Those poor fuckers have light blasting into their eyes 24/7. It's called torture, and I wasn't about to let you assholes do it to me."

"It wasn't meant as torture, Frank." But as he said the words, he wasn't so sure.

The man laughed, a raspy bark with an edge of cruelty. It made Thor's skin crawl. "You haven't learned a thing, have you, Anderssen? After everything that's happened, you still insist on seeing the best in people."

He sounded closer than Thor had expected, but that had to be an illusion. *The sailor couldn't be moving—could he?* Frank was tied up. Taking a step closer to the door, Thor held the sandwich plate in front of him like a peace offering. He was beginning to wish he'd brought a weapon. "I don't know about that. I don't see the best in you anymore."

Frank laughed again. "True enough. But you were fool enough to come down here on your own. I'm surprised the captain sent a boy to do a man's job. Where's Tomkins?"

Thor's throat felt as if it were choked with dust. He forced himself to swallow. "On deck. He's sick."

"Ah. Poor bastard finally told you, did he? I knew he wouldn't be able to hide it for long."

Cold sweat trickled down Thor's brow, even though the hold was stifling. He took another step toward the door. "Hide what? He has the flu."

"He doesn't have the flu, you idiot—he's dying. Take a gander at his ankle the next time you see him. That is, if there's anything left to see."

"What are you—?"

Something shifted in the darkness. Thor felt Frank's hot stinking breath on his face.

In that moment, he understood. Frank shouldn't have been able to move, but then again, he shouldn't have been able to talk, either. What had happened to his gag?

Thor realized his mistake too late.

"Sleep well, pretty boy."

Something hit the side of his head, hard. The clanging of metal reverberated in his ears and he had a brief moment of unbearable pain before the floor rushed to greet him.

CHAPTER TWENTY-THREE

He's free. You have to get out of there NOW.

The shriek woke Flora. She gasped as she struggled to get her bearings, heart pounding. She'd fallen asleep in the messdeck.

The last thing she remembered was Thor leaving to get Archie. They were going to bring Frank his lunch. But it felt like that had been a long time ago. Something had woken her, something that was making her mind roil with worry. What was it? What had she heard?

He's free. Get in the cooler and hide while you can. Move it.

Flora didn't stop to wonder who the voice belonged to. She rushed to the walk-in cooler in the galley, which was as good a place to hide as any. Fumbling with the handle, her hands were damp with sweat by the time she got the door open.

She blinked as she became accustomed to the dim light, yanking the door shut behind her. Searching the cooler for something large enough to conceal her body, she was frantic to turn off the light as soon as possible. If she kept it on, it would be a giveaway someone was hiding there.

At this stage in the journey, the cooler's provisions were sadly depleted. Doing the best she could, she snapped off the light and ducked behind a large bag of buckwheat flour in the far corner, banging her shin only once as she made her way in the dark.

No one on the crew was much for baking, so the bag was still bulky enough to hide her from view. She only hoped it wasn't full of vermin. Curling into a ball, she tucked her knees to her chest and shivered. Before she'd turned off the light, she'd been able to see her breath—*must remember to hold it if someone came in.*

If someone came in. Flora wasn't used to obeying strange commands yelled at her from within her own mind. She was going to feel ridiculous if one of the guys found her hiding in the cooler for no reason.

But something told her it was for a very good reason. Whatever it was, she trusted it.

* * *

Though she was no longer tired, Flora slipped into another nap. She snapped awake when she heard voices outside the cooler door.

"What did you do with Anderssen?"

"Don't worry, Captain. I treated your precious boy much better than you've treated me."

Fear wound its freezing hands around her heart and squeezed. Frank was supposed to be secured in the hold. How did he get out? Apostolos sounded furious, but she could hear the nerves beneath his fury. And that scared her more than anything.

"What about Tomkins?"

"Archie wasn't brain-dead enough to go down there. He's had no part of any of this, and that's the reason I'll let him live. Not that he has much time left, anyway."

What was he talking about? What's wrong with Archie? He was paler than usual, and maybe a little quiet, but she'd thought it was because of Frank.

"Don't be an idiot, Hearne. You don't want to spend the rest of your days in the brig."

Frank chuckled, and it was the most chilling sound she'd ever heard. It was the laugh of a man on the edge of madness.

"I have no fear of the brig, as you well know. I've done my time, and if I have to do a little more, so be it. Are you delusional enough to think any of us are going to survive that long? We're being picked off one by one, and you know it."

"Anderssen is going to get us out of here. He has a plan— unless you killed him."

Thor, dead? Flora pressed her hands to her lips to keep from crying out. It couldn't be true.

"And what does it matter if I did? Every one of us is going to be killed, sooner or later, and my vote is sooner. You're lucky to die by my hand instead of waiting for that creature to take you. Unless you'd rather be eaten alive from the inside out, like Archie."

"Tomkins is fine, Hearne. You don't know what you're talking about."

"Oh, don't I? Get him to show you his ankle, Captain. Although I imagine it's reached his leg by now—maybe even his hip. God knows Lashay didn't have long to wait."

Flora thought again of Archie, and how quiet the man had been lately. But the creature hadn't touched him.

"Enough chitchat, Captain. Either I shoot you now, or I can throw you overboard. You were fond of that idea when you were considering what to do with me, so it's only fair to offer you the same."

"I'll take my chances with the ocean," Apostolos said, and he was calm again, as if he were announcing what he'd like for lunch. "It's a fitting way for an old sailor to die. More honorable than being gunned down by the likes of you."

Flora heard a *click.* She bit her lip to keep from screaming.

"Watch it, Captain. I don't need much provoking. Before we send you off to Davy Jones, I need to know one thing—where's the cunt?"

Apostolos sputtered. "I don't know what you're talking about."

"Sure you do. There's only one cunt with legs on this ship. So where is she? Where are you hiding her?"

"If you're referring to Duchovney, I haven't seen her since lunch time. Maybe she's on deck."

"I thought no one was allowed on deck."

"I can't control what the crew does, and you're a perfect example of that. Wherever Duchovney is, she didn't check in with me, but she can't be far."

She didn't release the breath she was holding until she heard the men leave the mess, heading for the steps that would lead them to the deck—and Apostolos's death.

Her mind swam with so many questions she felt dizzy. For a minute, Flora forgot how cold she was. Where had Frank gotten a gun? She hadn't been aware of any weapons on board, except the harpoon. And how had he gotten loose? She prayed he hadn't killed Thor.

Most importantly, what should she do? She couldn't let Frank murder Apostolos, but she'd already been treated to an example of the man's strength, and knew she couldn't overpower him by herself. If she provided a distraction, perhaps Apostolos could take him down. The Greek was more than strong enough.

Grabbing hold of a shelf, she pulled herself to a standing position, wincing at the stiffness in her joints. Every part of her felt creaky and burned with cold. She scanned the cooler for a weapon. There were giant jars of pickles and industrial-sized cans of tuna, but she wasn't confident she could throw either of them with accuracy. Settling for the wooden handle of the push broom, she leaned against the cooler door, using her body weight to ease it open.

Except it didn't open.

Dropping the broom, Flora used both hands to push against the door.

It didn't budge.

The handle was broken. She was going to freeze to death among the last of the crew's provisions.

Trapped in the airtight cooler, Flora had only one weapon available to her, and she wasn't at all sure it would work.

But she had to try.

CHAPTER TWENTY-FOUR

Please help. He's going to kill the captain.

I was enjoying a nice light meal of blue algae with my wife when the scientist's voice blasted through my brain. Grimacing, I shook my head. I preferred my limited interactions with humans to be one way, but my link to the geologist was proving to be much stronger than I'd thought. In spite of my better instincts, my mind reached out and found her. She was still in trouble, but even worse this time. If she didn't get warmth and air soon, she'd expire.

I shook my head again, this time in weariness. Even when I tried to help them, humans invariably self-destructed.

"What is it, dear? What's troubling you?" Draugen's tone was sweet enough, but her eyes narrowed. Ever since her attack on the ship, I'd been spending the majority of my time with her and The Boy in an effort to placate them. My strategy appeared to be working. My son hardly ever whined about wanting the ship anymore, but my wife's expression showed she hadn't forgotten a thing. She was merely biding her time, as I was. Why hadn't these miserable creatures fixed their damn boat yet? I could only hold Draugen off for so long. Every day that ship remained in our territory, the angrier she got.

"It's the humans, isn't it? You're still obsessed with them."

"The humans? No, no, not at all. It's those giant clams we had earlier. They're not sitting right with me." I belched for effect, which wasn't difficult after such a huge meal.

My wife wrinkled her snout. "They were probably poisoned. Those horrible humans are poisoning everything these days."

She turned away, giving me an opportunity to answer the scientist when a sharp pain stabbed through my brain. Quickly I imagined a wall of coral slamming down. It snapped the probing lance in two with not a moment to spare.

"You are hiding something from me, Nøkken. What is it? I thought we'd agreed to have no more secrets from each other." My wife's upper lip curled, exposing fangs that were three times longer than my own.

"Reading my mind is a cheap trick, dearheart. You know I don't care for it, and beyond that, it's painful. What reason have I ever given you not to trust me?"

Help. We're running out of time. The captain will die. Frank is going to throw him overboard.

The new message shrilled across my brain, but this time I was ready for it and managed to keep my expression neutral as I shot off a reply.

Who are you to ask for my help? What is it to me if another one of you dies? You are no more than vermin to me. We were living in temples and palaces when you were still amoebae crawling around, spreading your disease.

I'd had more faith in the scientist than I should have—my wife was right. This woman was only another human, same as the rest. Even after I'd warned her, all she wanted was more of my help. Take, take, take. That's what they did.

I'm really sorry, but I don't know who else to turn to. I'm trapped in the cooler, and the captain is the only one who can run the ship. I know you want us to leave, and without him, we'll be stuck here.

That gave me pause.

If your captain enters the ocean, he won't die by my hand. We will let him be. Surely one of you can figure out a way to get him on the ship.

My son yanked me by the tail hard enough to draw blood. *Ouch. Impertinent little bugger.*

"Dad, let's do something. This is boring."

"Your father is busy with the humans again. Aren't you, Nøkken? There's no use lying to us. I can hear that female's screaming from here."

It hadn't occurred to me that Flora was powerful enough to transmit her thoughts to Draugen as well. Against my better nature, I issued a warning to her while I contemplated biting my son's head off.

You need to calm down. My wife can hear you, and believe me, you don't want to deal with her.

The reply blasted back immediately, and this time we both winced. Only our son was unaffected.

If he goes in the water, he'll drown. Or get eaten by sharks. He'll die for sure. We're running out of time. You're our last hope. PLEASEHELPPLEASEHELPPLEASEHELP.

"She's a mouthy little thing, isn't she? You should tell her to keep her voice down if you don't want me to hear."

"This is the first time she's done this, Draugen, I swear."

"And I wonder how she knew she could. You've been teaching her, I suppose?" My wife circled me while my son followed, smirking. He clearly thought this was a game. Or perhaps he knew his father wasn't long for this world and was thrilled that my wife's attention would soon be focused solely on him.

"Not at all. You think I want the inane chatter of humans in my ears?"

HELP.

"That's it." My wife snarled. "I'm getting rid of that boat."

"Yay!" My son spun in circles, snapping at passing fish.

"Wait a minute." I realized I could relieve my wife's rage and aid the geologist at the same time. "We have to be strategic about this."

Draugen rolled her eyes. "Really, Nøkken—I'm growing weary of your games. These are humans like any other. They don't deserve special consideration."

"Oh? Have you ever had one communicate with you before?"

My wife didn't have to answer. For whatever reason, the scientist was an anomaly. Maybe she would turn out to be as bad as the rest of her kin, but maybe not. It was worth giving her a chance.

"Her communication leaves a lot to be desired. I'd be just as happy never to hear from her again."

"She's panicking," I said, scarcely able to believe I was defending her. "The one man who can steer the ship and get them out of our territory is in danger."

"I can get every single one of them out of our territory in about five seconds," Draugen said with a grin that would have made my blood run cold—if I wasn't already cold-blooded.

"We need the humans to get their boat to shore so they can warn the others, remember? If they disappear, the rest of their tribe will come searching for them." There was nothing people loved more than an unsolved mystery. It was one of the main reasons we'd had to leave our beloved Bermuda Triangle.

"What are you asking of me? Surely you don't expect me to float my days away, snacking on algae, while they clutter our territory and our minds."

"No—on the contrary, I think you *should* go. But we need to have a plan."

As fast as I could, I described the one they called "Frank Hearne" to my wife—dirty, nasty man that he was.

That little bastard was about to get a lesson in karma. Too bad it wouldn't last very long.

CHAPTER TWENTY-FIVE

Thor woke in darkness. Fetid, foul-smelling darkness.

He blinked, not sure his eyes were open, and then was sorry he had. The pain ricocheted across his forehead before settling behind his eyes with a nasty throb.

Extending his arm, he searched for whatever it was that had knocked him out. He was pretty sure he'd heard it hit the floor a moment before he had. It wasn't long before his hands closed around a wooden handle. His fingers worked their way along until they came to the business end.

Thor moaned when he realized what it was. *A sledgehammer.* They'd left a fucking sledgehammer in a room with a mad, captive sailor. There was no limit to their idiocy. Of course, they hadn't expected Frank to escape, but in hindsight, that was pretty damn stupid too.

Frank. Even though it felt like his head would shatter into a million pieces, Thor staggered to his feet. Thankfully the sailor hadn't taken the time to restrain him, but Thor wasn't sure whether or not he should be offended by that.

God knows how long Frank had been out there and what havoc he'd wreaked during that time. His stint in the hold must have driven him mad. If he got his hands on Flora again, he'd probably kill her.

* * *

Thor shuffled to the upper decks, the sledgehammer held in front of him like an absurd dowsing rod. Without the engine running, the ship was eerily silent. Soon he realized he couldn't hear the hum of the generator, either. *Fuck. Couldn't they keep anything going without me?* Of course, they probably had other things on their minds.

When Thor reached the messdeck, he looked for Flora, almost expecting to see her sitting at the table where he'd left her. But the ship's kitchen was empty. There were no signs of a struggle, or blood on the floor. He tried to take comfort in that.

"You're dooming everyone on the ship."

It was Apostolos, yelling from the upper deck.

Thor tightened his grip on the sledgehammer.

Showtime.

* * *

"Get over yourself. If a moron like you can manage her, I'm sure I can figure it out."

"You don't understand. This ship is different. It takes special training—"

Apostolos spotted Thor as he crept onto the deck. His eyes flicked to him for only a second—half a second—but it was enough. Frank spun around, his eyes crazed. He was holding a gun.

"Ha, beautiful. Boy Wonder's come to save the day. You didn't put up much of a fight down below, though, did ya?"

"It doesn't take much skill to hit someone with a sledgehammer when they can't see you coming."

Thor knew he wouldn't have been a match for Frank, even if the men had fought hand to hand in bright daylight, but there was no way he'd admit that. Thankfully, Apostolos hadn't lost any of his wits. While Frank was distracted, the big Greek seized the gun.

Frank held fast, and soon both men were engaged in a frantic tug-of-war. Archie leaned against the bow nearby, looking worse than ever. There was no point appealing to him for help. Continuing his painful progress across the deck, Thor hoped he'd be able to get in a good shot at Frank. The Greek's arm muscles bulged and strained with the effort of holding on to the weapon, but he wasn't about to let go. The men appeared to be evenly matched.

Thor raised the sledgehammer with both hands and waited for an opening, arms trembling. For now, the adrenaline pumping through his veins kept the pain at bay, but he knew he'd pay for this later. The collar of his shirt was crusted with dried blood that crackled whenever he moved his head. Frank hadn't given him a love tap, but thankfully he hadn't put his arm into it either.

The Greek fell to the deck with Frank underneath him, but the captain didn't have the chance to land a single punch before the grizzled sailor shifted positions. Apostolos tore the gun from Frank's hands during the struggle, and Thor managed to kick it out of reach. He had to hop to the side to keep from being mowed down by the rolling duo. Still clutching the sledgehammer, but lower now, he watched for an opportunity. If he missed and hit Apostolos, it would be worse than doing nothing.

Distracted as Thor was, he didn't notice the ocean was unusually calm, as if the world were holding its breath.

The creature burst out of the water behind the struggling men. Thor stumbled backward, unable to take his eyes off it. It resembled a brontosaurus with a much longer neck, but its teeth were more like a T-rex's. Its small eyes were yellow and filled with hate—yes, hate. There was no doubt in Thor's mind that this was a sentient creature. The sledgehammer tumbled from his hands and he fell, landing hard on his butt, the agony blasting through his skull enough to make him scream. He could barely hear himself over Frank and Apostolos, who were both yelling.

Frank rolled off the Greek and ran for the stairs, but the creature was too fast. With one twitch of its neck, it had the sailor in its jaws. Thor pressed his face to the deck, but he could hear the horrible crunching as the creature tore into Frank. The sailor's screams stopped as quickly as they'd begun.

There was stillness, and then a dull thump. No one moved. Thor felt a sensation, almost like a warm breeze, pass over his body, and before he knew what was happening, his bladder let go. He fully expected to die, but after a minute had passed, he risked a look.

Apostolos was lying on the deck as if pinned, staring in terror at the creature, who was glaring back at him.

THIS IS YOUR LAST WARNING. FIX YOUR BOAT AND LEAVE OUR TERRITORY. DO NOT RETURN. TELL OTHERS

OF YOUR KIND THEY ARE NOT WELCOME HERE. IF WE SEE ANOTHER HUMAN, WE WILL NOT BE SO MERCIFUL.

The words exploded in Thor's brain as if he'd turned his iPod past the highest setting. Clapping his hands to his ears, he groaned, nauseous with pain, but Apostolos just nodded, stricken, his eyes locked on the creature.

Then it was gone, as silently as it had arrived.

Apostolos got to his feet. "Anderssen, are you all right?"

Thor was, until he saw Frank. Or what was left of him. The sailor's head had been separated from his body, tumbling across the deck until it was a few feet away. The man's eyes were dazed, as if he wasn't sure what hit had him.

Thor heard someone screaming. It was a while before he realized the sound was coming from his own throat.

CHAPTER TWENTY-SIX

The sound of metal scratching against the door snapped Flora out of her daze. She pushed aside the sack of grain, almost crying with relief.

But then she froze.

What if Frank had won?

When the door swung wide, blinding her with the warm light from the messdeck, she collapsed into Apostolos's arms, unable to hold back her tears.

At first the big man seemed startled, but then he returned her embrace. "I'm sorry, Duchovney. I didn't expect to take this long. You must be half-frozen."

She laughed, wiping away her tears. "No half about it. I'm a Popsicle. I'm just glad you're okay."

He helped her to a chair and wrapped the tablecloth around her shivering body. "Aye, I'm fine. I can't say the same for Hearne, though."

"Is he in the hold?" The thought of Frank made her tremble even harder.

"No, he's in the ocean."

Apostolos collapsed into the nearest chair, clutching several bottles of beer. He offered one to her, but she shook her head. "You'll forgive me if I get roaring drunk. It's either that or go crazy."

Flora closed her eyes in relief. Her plan must have worked—the creature must have heard her and decided to help. Why, she had no idea, but she figured it had its own reasons.

A part of her felt guilty for condemning Frank to such a death. It was her fault he was gone, as if she'd murdered him with her own hands. But she didn't see what choice she'd had. It was either him or everyone else.

"Where's Thor?"

"He went to lie down. He took a good whack on the head with a sledgehammer." Apostolos drained half of his first bottle in a single gulp. "I don't imagine he's feeling too good."

"A *sledgehammer?* Are you sure he's okay?"

The Greek nodded, wiping his mouth. "He'll be fine. He was lucky. From what I understand, Hearne had the lights off when Anderssen went to feed him, which was a lucky break. If Hearne could have seen well enough to get a clean shot, he would have cracked that skull right open."

Flora rubbed her arms to warm them, the tingling in her fingers almost unbearable. She worried about her friend. What if he had a concussion? She'd always heard you should keep people awake when they were concussed. What if Thor slipped into a coma? She felt helpless. The only person on the crew with any medical training was fish food now.

"If you wouldn't mind, maybe once he's awake you can take care of him, help him clean his head," Apostolos said, not meeting her eyes. "I'm not much good at that kind of thing."

She didn't think she was either, but she'd be happy to help Thor. "Of course. I'll do what I can. What about Archie?"

In response, Apostolos opened another beer, cracking the cap off on the edge of the table. "I couldn't get him off the deck. Not even after what happened. He's cowering by the bow. He saw the whole damn thing." The Greek took another long swallow. "Maybe you can see to him too."

Whatever strange connection she had with the creature told her it was gone. It was safe on the deck for now, but it wasn't a great idea for Archie to get comfortable hanging around there. Perhaps he was frightened and needed someone to talk to. It was worth a try.

She had started to leave when Apostolos reached for her arm. He shook his head. "Not yet. Let me finish this beer, and I'll swab the deck. You don't want to walk past that."

Flora sank into her chair. No, she didn't. After everything else that had happened, she wasn't sure she could handle it. Her hands hurt from their stint in the cooler, and she tucked them under her arms to warm them.

Apostolos laughed as he finished his last beer, but his expression betrayed his despair. "We're quite the mess, aren't we? At the rate we're going, by the time we get this rig working again, there won't be anyone left to rescue."

She forced a smile as he left the table, but knew it was as false as his laugh.

CHAPTER TWENTY-SEVEN

"How are you feeling?"

Something cool and soft pressed against his forehead. It didn't slow the marching band that was determined to bash its way through his skull, but he appreciated the gesture.

"I've been better." He was thankful for the darkness—thankful she couldn't see how weak his attempt at a smile was.

"I don't doubt it. Is there anything I can get for you?"

"Do we have any more of that aspirin left from Frank's stash?"

"I think so. I'll go get it."

"Wait—can you stay with me awhile?"

"Of course." She sounded surprised. "But it won't take me long to get the pills. They're in my cabin."

"Okay." He let her go, trying to ignore the flutter of panic he felt when the room was empty. But that was ridiculous, wasn't it? Hearne was gone; the monster would leave them alone. *For now.* What was there to be afraid of?

Flora had left the cabin door open. He could see the light from her room and hear the rustling as she pawed through the bag. She returned to his side within a minute, pressing the chalky pills and a plastic water bottle into his hand.

"Thanks."

"Do you need any help?"

Thor was about to say no before he saw that he did. "If you could help me sit up, that would be great."

It hurt like hell to move his head the slightest bit, and even though he had two pillows supporting him, the sweat ran down his face. When Flora gently moved him forward, she touched his collar. She gasped.

"You're not okay, are you?"

"I'll be fine," he said, trying his best to sound more confident than he felt. He took a swig of water. It was on the warm side, but was still the best thing he'd ever tasted. "I'll be fine when the aspirin kicks in."

"You've lost a lot of blood."

"I'm okay, Mom—I promise." He immediately wished he could take it back. Flora hadn't been anything but kind. "Sorry. I didn't mean that to sound as snarky as it did."

"That's okay. I *was* mothering you. It's just…Apostolos asked me to take care of you, and I'm not a doctor. Mothering is the only experience I have with this sort of thing."

"Fair enough. I guess everybody has been shoved out of their comfort zone on this trip."

"Now *that's* the understatement of the year."

He grinned, but even that small movement felt like it would tear his skin from his scalp. He couldn't let Flora find out how bad his injury was—she'd only worry. Hell, *he* didn't want to know how bad it was. "I guess Frank wasn't the pushover we thought."

"I never thought he was a pushover. Did you?"

"You have a point. But I sure didn't expect the bugger to attack me."

"Why didn't you take Archie with you?" Before Thor could respond, she held up her hand. "I'm not giving you shit; I'm just curious."

"He wouldn't go." He thought of Archie's pale face, his vomit-stained shirt. At the time Thor had felt sorry for him, but now he was angry. "Some bullshit about being too sick. He probably knew what his buddy had in store for me, and didn't want to see it."

"I don't think Archie would let you walk into something like that," Flora said. "He's a good man."

"I don't know about that. Something's wrong with him."

"Maybe he *is* sick. Apostolos wants me to check on him once I'm done here, but he told me he wanted to—" she paused, lowering her eyes. "Swab the deck first."

Thor's stomach lurched as he tried not to picture Frank's last moments. "Your buddy sure did a hell of a job."

"My buddy?"

He heard the edge in her voice and knew he'd offended her again. *Shit.* Wasn't there some Get Out of Jail Free card for guys who'd been knocked on the head? He wasn't Mister Smooth at the best of times, but now he was tripping over himself like a dog on roller skates. "Sorry, didn't mean anything by it. The sea creature." He'd started to say monster, but caught himself in time.

"I know what you meant."

"Oh come on, Flora—everyone knows you're linked to the creature in some way. I'm not Frank, for Chrissake. I'm not going to call you a witch and throw you overboard."

Her mouth twitched. "Thank God for small favors."

"Wait—was that an actual *smile?*"

Sadly, it vanished as swiftly as it had appeared. "I'm not the Ice Queen you guys make me out to be, you know."

"Of course not. But can't a man get a little slack? A sledgehammer-wielding sailor scrambled my brains. I'm lucky I can remember my own name."

She smiled again—for real this time. "You're right; I'm sorry. I'm still processing this, I guess. Nothing like this has ever happened to me before."

"I think it's safe to say you're not alone there."

"But it's different for me." Flora eased herself onto the end of the bed, careful not to jostle him. "I can hear the creature's voice in my head. I can even argue with him, have conversations, and I have no idea why this is happening. I thought I was imagining it, but that was wishful thinking. Whatever the cause, it's truly bizarre." She glanced over her shoulder. "Please don't tell the other guys. I'm ostracized enough."

"I think everyone who ostracized you is no longer with us," Thor said, not understanding the panic that came over her face until she spoke.

"I had nothing to do with what happened to Liam or George. You have to believe me."

"The thought never entered my mind." Though it had, at least a little bit. "Liam and George didn't do anything to you. But Frank?"

She closed her eyes for a moment, breathing deeply. "I don't like to think about it. But we had no choice. If I hadn't reached out for help, Frank would have killed Apostolos. And me along with him."

"We would have figured something out."

"Really? You were badly hurt and Archie wouldn't leave the deck."

Thor was quiet for a moment, considering her predicament. He understood why she'd felt such desperation, though he wasn't sure he could have doomed Frank to such a fate, no matter how big a threat the sailor was. Frank hadn't tried to rape him, of course, but he'd made a fair attempt to kill him. Even so, it wasn't that easy a call. He remembered how hard the sailor had fought to save Liam.

Thor was grateful he wasn't God—he had no desire for that kind of power.

"You're not the only one who can hear it, you know."

Flora's eyes widened. "Are you saying you can too?"

"The Greek and I both heard it warn us off after it put an end to poor Frank. If you can still get messages across, I'd appreciate a slight extension on the deadline. I'm not sure when I'm going to be in diving shape."

"How long do you think you'll need?"

He heard the fear in her voice. As much as he'd attempted to convince himself, it was obvious he wasn't going to be fixing anything for a while. Especially when the only medication he had access to was aspirin. And not even the extra-strength kind.

"I'm not sure. A few days at least."

"It wasn't him," Flora said in a quiet voice, staring at her hands.

"What are you talking about? What wasn't him?"

"The one who killed Frank and George—the creature that gave you the warning. It's not the same one I can communicate with."

His head pounded. "There are *more* of them?"

Flora nodded. "The one who killed Frank was his mate. From what I gather, his wife is larger and more aggressive. She also has a real hate-on for humans. I don't get the feeling he's a fan, either, but he's more—civilized, for lack of a better word."

"Wow." Thor was stunned. "The female of the species is deadlier than the male."

"In this case, yes. And he doesn't have much control over her, so while I can reach out to him about the timeline, I can't make any promises." She ran a hand through her hair, tugging on it as if she wanted to rip it out. "Do you hear how crazy this sounds? I just told you I'd try to telepathically communicate with a previously unknown sea creature, so I can talk him out of killing us. Is this actually happening?"

He was too shocked by her latest revelation to reassure her. "If there are two, there could be more."

"Yes."

"But where are they? I mean, how come no one has ever seen them before? They're too massive to hide for long."

"Maybe people don't tend to survive seeing them. But then again, there's so much we don't know about the ocean. Why do you think I became a marine geologist? The *ocean* is the final frontier."

Thor's head felt like it was about to crack open, and not from Frank's attack. "I don't know how to deal with this. Sea monsters belong in fairytales, not real life."

"They're only monsters because we don't know anything about them. If you think about it, almost everything was a monster at some point."

Remembering how George and then Frank had been ripped apart, Thor shuddered. As far as he was concerned, it was the creatures' behavior that made them monsters more than anything else.

"I think I'm going to sleep for a little while," he said. "I have to build my strength if I'm going to fix the boat."

Flora slid off the mattress as quickly as if he'd pushed her. "Of course—I'm sorry, what was I thinking? You should rest."

"Thanks for checking on me." His eyes drifted closed. The company had been nice, but what he wanted now, more than anything, was to be left alone.

"Any time. Once you're feeling stronger, we'll get you cleaned up." Flora said something else, but it didn't register.

He was already gone.

CHAPTER TWENTY-EIGHT

The ship had an abandoned feel to it that made Flora uneasy as she left Thor's darkened cabin for the gloomy passageway. There were so few of the crew left. She almost missed Frank's ribald sense of humor and George's griping.

Even the messdeck, her former safe place, wasn't inviting anymore. She imagined someone waiting there, watching her, as she hurried past, but she knew that was impossible. Still, she was grateful to reach the stairs to the deck.

"Apostolos?" she called, weak with relief when the Greek answered.

"Yes, go ahead. It's okay now."

But nothing was okay. She could feel how pitted and rough the wood was under her feet now. Flora tried not to think about what that meant, but she knew. She was walking over the place Frank had died.

The fire-orange sun was setting, lending the deck a lovely glow, but she was too worried to appreciate it. She could make out Archie's silhouette slumped over the bow.

"No change?" she whispered, and the Greek shook his head, his eyes watery.

"If anything, he's worse. What happened to Frank hasn't done him any favors. Will you talk to him? See if you can get him to eat something?"

He must have seen the reluctance on her face, because he touched her shoulder before she could leave. "I know neither of us are nursemaid types, but you have to admit your bedside manner is a cut above mine. Anderssen can't take care of himself right now, let alone anyone else."

"I'll see what I can do."

She dragged her feet as she crossed the deck to stand beside Archie. He didn't acknowledge her approach, and for a moment, she wondered if he realized she was there. The big man hung partly over the side of the boat, staring at the water. The color was gone from his skin, though he'd been in the sun all day.

"You don't have to talk to me," he said, so quietly that for a minute she wasn't sure she'd heard him.

"I know I don't *have* to. I want to." She tried to sound cheery, but her voice came across flat, even to her own ears. The truth was, Archie didn't smell too good. It wasn't only the vomit crusted on his shirt or the rank musk of a man who hadn't bathed or brushed his teeth in a while. He smelled like something rotting.

"You don't have to lie to me. I know Apostolos told you to come over here and check on me. Man never could stand to do his own dirty work." The last sentence was muttered under Archie's breath.

"I'd hardly call you dirty work, Archie." When he didn't respond, she took a deep breath and tried again. "I've heard you've been feeling sick. Can you tell me what's wrong?"

He turned to face her, and the change in him was so great that she bit her lip to keep from reacting. Archie had always been a jovial sort whose eyes sparkled with humor even when he was quiet. Not anymore. Now they were bloodshot and sunken and filled with a resigned sadness. They were the eyes of a man who wanted to be left alone. "Nothing you can help me with," he said before looking back at the water.

"I know I don't have medical training, and I'm sorry Frank's not here, but there might be something I can do to help. I need you to tell me what's wrong."

"I don't blame you, Flora. Frank was a different man at the end. I know he had to die," Archie said to the ocean. "I may not like what you did, but I understand why you thought you had no choice."

She felt like she'd been slapped. Her shoulders stiffened. "Don't blame me for what? I don't know what you're talking about."

"Sure you do. You don't have to play dumb with me. Those things have touched me now too, so I know. I can hear them. I heard what they said to you. I know you asked them to kill Frank."

Flora shivered, chilled in spite of the warm air. "I didn't ask them to kill Frank. I asked them to help us."

"Yeah, and they knew what you meant by that, same as I did. I'm not as dumb as I look."

"I'm sorry we needed their help, and I'm not happy Frank's gone. I'm not happy anything turned out this way." She beckoned at Apostolos, but the Greek made an impatient *Go on* gesture at her, staying where he was. *Coward.* She clenched her teeth. If he was so concerned about Archie, why wasn't he here? Why was he hiding on the other side of the deck?

"I just wanted you to know there are no hard feelings between you and me. I've always believed a man should say everything there is to say before he dies."

"Please, Archie—you're not dying. As soon as Thor feels stronger, he's going to fix the ship. We'll be home in a few days, and you'll get the medical care you need."

"Didn't I tell you that you don't need to lie to me? I *am* dying. I know it, and I think you know it as well." He gripped the side of the bow with both hands, leaning out a little farther. What was left of his dark hair blew crazily in the wind. Flora realized he was much thinner on top than he used to be. Was it the stress of the last week, or had Archie pulled out his own hair? "The only question is whether I'm going to choose my own death or let it be chosen for me."

Oh my God. That's why he keeps standing out here. He's working up the nerve to jump.

It had been a while since Flora had had a man in her life, but her son was a constant reminder of how stubborn they could be. Rather than continue the pointless argument, she decided on a new approach. "Can you tell me why you think you're going to die?"

"I can do better than that. I'll show you." Before she could react, Archie yanked the leg of his jeans to his knee. The smell of rot was so overpowering she stumbled back, retching.

His ankle was a bubbling, foaming mess. The flesh was coming away from the bone in shreds. Blood and a horrible greenish liquid oozed from the wound.

Overcome with dizziness, her head spinning, Flora felt her legs go out from under her but was powerless to stop it. There was nothing to grab. She hit the deck with a thump. Behind her, she could hear Apostolos's boots thudding on the planks as he rushed to close the distance between them.

Archie, who had been defiant, even angry, seconds before, now burst into tears. He dropped his pant leg and turned to the water, his shoulders shaking.

"My God, man. When did this happen to you?"

Flora went weak with relief. Apostolos had seen it too—he would figure it out. Her stomach roiled, and she crawled to the side of the ship to vomit.

"A couple days ago. At first it was only a tiny spot. I thought it was a blister." Archie's voice cracked. "But it got worse and worse."

"Why didn't you tell us?" Apostolos gave Archie a little shake.

"What would have been the point? I know what this means. And you had your hands full with Frank and getting the ship and the generator going again. You didn't need to waste your time on a dying man."

"You are *not* going to die, Tomkins."

Flora returned to the men on shaky legs, wiping her mouth on her sleeve. For a moment, she thought she must have heard Apostolos wrong.

"That ankle is going to need to come off, though. Maybe if you'd told us sooner, we could have saved it. But if we get moving now, we might be able to save most of the leg."

Archie flattened himself against the bow, looking as horrified as Flora felt. "You can't cut off my ankle."

"Your ankle or your life, Tomkins. That's the choice, and I am *not* letting another man die on this ship. There's been too much death already."

"Captain?"

She thought Apostolos might snap at her, but instead he only sighed. "Yes, Duchovney? What is it?"

"I don't want Archie to die, either. But this isn't a sterile environment. We don't have the proper equipment, and we don't have anything to prevent infection. If you try to amputate his ankle, he's only going to get gangrene...or worse." She touched Archie gently on the shoulder, and when the man didn't pull away, rubbed his arm in the hopes of soothing him. His trembling made her want to weep, but she fought to keep her emotions in check.

"And there's nothing to knock me out with. I don't think I could stand that. As it is now, the pain isn't so bad," Archie said, greasy beads of sweat running down his face. "I'd rather wait here until it gets to a point where I can't stand it, then let one of those buggers take me. Let them finish what they started."

"Oh, I'll knock you out, Tomkins. You don't have to worry about that." Apostolos squinted at Flora. "We must have some rubbing alcohol in one of those first-aid kits."

She shook her head. "We used almost everything we had on Liam. We have a little bit of aspirin left, but between Archie and Thor, it's not going to stretch very far."

"She's right, Captain. I appreciate the thought, but I've already accepted my fate, and this is the way I'd rather go."

"You're not going anywhere, goddammit. That ankle is coming off now, and you'll be fine. We'll bring this barge home in a couple of days, and rush you to a hospital." He clapped Archie on the shoulder again, harder this time. "You're going to be fine." The Greek focused his attention on Flora. "And you will help me. You aren't squeamish, are you? I mean, you're a scientist, right? You must have done dissections and such."

She wanted to tell him that dissecting the remains of a poor, pickled little creature in the lab was a far cry from butchering a man she knew—a man who was still alive. But her mouth had gone dry. Instead, she nodded, and her heart fell as she saw a new emotion creep into Archie's eyes.

Hope.

CHAPTER TWENTY-NINE

In spite of her ferocious appetite, my wife was what humans would call a "homebody." As the male, I did the hunting, and usually the only time she ventured out was when I hadn't fed her enough. When that happened, I had to be on my guard; she was bound to be nippy when she returned.

So when my wife prepared to leave the lair in the early morning with a pleased expression on her face, I was wary. I liked the smirk on my son's pointy face even less. Clearly they had something planned.

"Where are you off to, dearheart?" I strived to sound casual.

She smiled, displaying her impressive teeth. "The Boy and I are going to visit the surface."

My son ran his long tongue over his own teeth while he grinned at me. How I longed to wipe that look off his face.

"The surface? Draugen, you haven't given them enough time. Their mechanic is still hurt—you know that. He can't possibly fix the ship until he's able to move around again."

Truthfully, I had little hope he would ever be able to repair it. From what the geologist's jumbled thoughts indicated, the young man had received a good crack on the head—hard enough to injure his brain, and probably enough to have killed a lesser human. Still, to destroy them now, without giving them a chance to fix their little craft, would be dishonorable.

"I warned them, Nøkken. I gave them a deadline. They have failed." Her tone was light, even jovial, but I could hear the unspoken warning behind it.

"Your deadline means nothing if they are not physically able to meet it." Her smile faded, which gave me a little hope. "Please let them be. They are no longer drilling. They are not making noise or harming our territory in any way. They're just drifting."

My wife flared her nostrils in a huff. "I don't like the smell of them."

"I don't much either, but surely we can stay downwind for a few more days. Then they can fix their ship, go home, and warn the others to stay away. In exchange for this inconvenience, we could have centuries of peace."

"That would be lovely. Do you really believe that?"

"I do." Privately, though, I had my doubts. Humans weren't much for heeding warnings, especially from other humans.

"You know I promised him that ship. He's getting antsy." Draugen indicated our son with a tilt of her head, and I glanced down to find him glaring at me. It was a fair imitation of his mother, and enough to make me cringe. I'd definitely have to get more involved in his upbringing.

"He has more than enough ships, Draugen. He's getting spoiled as it is."

At my words, our son bared his teeth in a growl. I pulled away, astonished. He'd pushed his boundaries before, but had never been so openly disrespectful. Even my wife gaped at him in shock.

"Boy, that's your father. Show some respect."

"Why do I have to show *him* any respect? He has none for me." The Boy's whiny voice set my teeth on edge, my irritation crossing over to fury. Was this what Draugen had been teaching him? Where did he think his dinner came from? I'd never seen such an ungrateful child, and I regretted protecting him from the great whites when he was little.

"Because he's your *father*. You're only a child," Draugen said, warning me with her eyes.

"I still count." Our son thrashed around the lair's entrance. Thankfully, he was too small to cause the same damage as his mother. "And you've been promising me that ship for weeks. It's only fair that I get it. You have no right to spoil this."

Before Draugen could speak, I stared down my angry child. "Well then, this is a perfect opportunity for you to learn a valuable life lesson, son."

His eyes narrowed into slits as he paused before me, puffing with exertion. "What lesson is that?"

"Life isn't fair."

He shrieked with rage, but by now I was enjoying this. Let him have his little temper tantrum, so long as I retained the upper hand.

"That's *stupid,*" he said.

I turned to his mother. "You see? Spoiled. I don't think he should ever get that ship, even if it's abandoned on the sea floor. He can't control himself in the face of disappointment."

Draugen hung her head. "Perhaps you're right."

The Boy regarded her with horror, his eyes wide and pleading. "But, Mom, you promised."

"I know I did, son, and that was my mistake. I'm very sorry, but we'll have to find you another toy. Your father is correct—I have not honored my agreement with the humans. It would be wrong to kill them and destroy their ship. They need it to return home."

If she thought her words would have any calming effect on our child, she soon discovered otherwise. He gnashed his fangs in exasperation, giving her a look of such disgust that I was astounded. He was only ten thousand years old. Why was he acting like a teenager already?

"They're just humans. No one will miss them."

Before I could think twice, my tail whipped forward and lashed my son across the face, sending him crashing into one of the coral walls, where an anemone promptly stung him.

Even though the acid in our veins doesn't dissolve our skin on contact, it still burns. I saw with some embarrassment that I'd cut my boy. Blood trickled down one cheek under his left eye. His mouth hung open in a comical expression of amazement, but he didn't challenge me further.

I turned to face Draugen, expecting her to tear me apart, but she didn't appear to be angry. Just sad.

"You shouldn't hit him for my mistakes, Nøkken. I'm the one who made him the way he is."

"Nonsense. You've been a good mother. But we need to teach him some respect now, while we still can. You know as well as I do that he's probably going to be bigger than both of us, and his cruelty frightens me."

She frowned. "I don't agree with corporal punishment."

"I don't either—as you know, dearheart. I can't explain my actions, I'm afraid. It was as if my tail had a mind of its own."

Draugen's face brightened, and for the first time in a long while, it felt like we were on the same team. "I suppose it's fine, this one time. But in the future, tell your tail to mind its own business."

"Of course. Excellent suggestion."

Seeing us laughing together, our son must have known he was beat. His greatest strength, I realized with a sudden chill, was turning my wife and me against each other, driving a wedge between us. He slunk off to his room, trailing a cloud of blood.

"Should I go after him?" I asked, not wanting to, but feeling guilty. We were the enlightened ones. If we started tearing each other apart, we'd be no better than humans.

"No, I'll check on him later. He needs to cool down first. I know you feel bad for striking him, but he never should have shown you such disrespect. Besides, it's only a scrape."

At her words, I felt the last bit of tension leave my body. After the emotional stress of the day, I wanted nothing more than to head to my den and sleep. Violence and conflict were not my forte, and there had been too much of both lately.

"In any case, he's learned his lesson," my wife continued.

"Really?" I asked, optimistic but doubtful.

"Most definitely. I've never seen him end an argument that quickly before. He usually needs to have the last word. This time, the last word was yours."

If only we'd known how wrong we were.

CHAPTER THIRTY

The Greek poured another liter of his good rum into the bucket, wincing at the sizzling that resulted.

Archie had passed out some time before, his mouth open as he snored. His leg was in a bucket filled with ice-cold water and alcohol. Apostolos hoped the freezing temperature would numb the area and slow down whatever was consuming the man's flesh. Flora wasn't sure how well it was working, mostly because she couldn't bear to look at Archie's foot.

It had taken some doing, but they'd finally convinced Archie that the best course of action was to remove his calf, leaving the kneecap intact. That way, they'd be sawing through tendons and soft tissue rather than bone, and there would be a bit of a barrier in case the sea creature's acid had spread.

"Are you ready for this?" the Greek asked, his eyes rimmed with red.

"I don't think I'll ever be ready, but best to do it when he's passed out."

Apostolos handed her the bottle of rum. She almost refused, but the thought of oblivion was tempting. The alcohol took her breath away, and she gasped as it ignited a path down her throat to her stomach.

The Greek waited for her, his hands under Archie's arms, ready to lift him from the chair. Flora tugged on a pair of thick rubber fisherman's gloves. She'd be carrying Archie's legs, which were lighter than his upper body, but also more dangerous. She couldn't let the poison touch her own skin, not even for a second. The very thought made her queasy.

She grasped Archie under the knees, turning her head so she didn't have to see his bloody stump. Then Apostolos lifted the unconscious man with a grunt, and all she could think about was keeping her balance as she struggled to follow him without knocking over the bucket or getting tangled in a chair. After a few long seconds, they reached Frank's old bunk and settled Archie upon it, trying their best not to disturb him.

Flora's hands shook as she helped Apostolos tie Archie to the bed with strips of old sheets and hang a shower curtain for her protection. Thor moaned in the other room. She was worried about the engineer, who spent most of his time asleep now, but at least that meant he didn't know what they were about to do to Archie. She envied his ignorance.

Apostolos slipped a plank under Archie's leg, and Flora grimaced upon seeing that the man's ankle was little more than bone with some shreds of flesh. Now that it was out of the bucket, the smell was unbearable. She felt her gorge rise.

"You sure you can handle this?" Apostolos asked, eying her with concern. He looked like a cross between a butcher and a doctor, which she guessed was appropriate. One of his shirts had been folded into a mask and tied around his face so only his eyes and brows were showing.

Unable to speak, she nodded.

"Remember, as soon as I tell you it's done, you have to apply the tourniquet to his leg and stop the bleeding. I'll cauterize the arteries. If we don't do everything right, we'll lose him." He leaned forward and gripped her shoulder with a powerful hand. "I need you with me, Duchovney. I can't do this alone."

She nodded again, swallowing the panic that fluttered in her stomach. She didn't have time for panic. "I was thinking…maybe some music?"

To her surprise, he appeared relieved. "That's a great idea. Choose something loud—something upbeat."

And that's how they came to amputate their friend's leg with the raucous sounds of Poison reverberating through the ship. She sent a silent apology to Thor, and a prayer to the creatures to leave them alone that night.

The last thing Flora saw before Apostolos drew the rubber curtain between them was the Greek pouring the last of his precious spiced rye over his crewmember's leg. His eyes were set and grim and completely sober.

At his signal, Flora stretched her body across the unconscious man's chest and held on with all her strength.

* * *

The saw sprang to life with a roar, and she wedged her face against the wall, willing herself not to look. She knew when Apostolos began to cut because the entire bed shuddered and Archie started to scream.

Flora tried her best to hold him, but it was like trying to calm a raging river. As Archie thrashed from side to side, shrieking in agony, she could hear Apostolos bellowing at her to keep him down. The saw made an awful clatter that was still much too audible over Bret Michaels's wails. She pressed her arms against her ears to block the sound and gritted her teeth, trying to think of something—anything—else. She pictured her son's face, and clung to the memory of his easy smile, his bright blue eyes. How she longed to be at home with him instead of in this living nightmare.

"Don't need nothin' but a good time—how can I resist?"

She retched at the smell that assaulted her from the other end of the bed, and cried out when Archie grabbed her foot, but managed to stay in control. Soon the roaring stopped and Flora knew Apostolos was using the chef's knife. The realization made her green. She clenched her teeth, drawing on some inner strength she hadn't known she possessed.

Archie went limp underneath her. The song ended, and she realized the Greek was talking to her. "Hurry, I need you *now.*"

She slid off Archie's unconscious body and rushed to the other side of the curtain. Apostolos held a wad of clean towels to Archie's leg—or what was left of it. When he saw her, he seized her gloved hands and put them where his had been.

"Use as much pressure as you can. Don't ease up, even for a second. I have to get rid of the leg. I'll be right back."

Flora pushed down on Archie's stump as if her life depended on it. It was less than a minute before Apostolos returned, but it felt like hours. What if Archie had regained consciousness and thrashed around again?

"I need you to hold him. I still have to cauterize the wound. *Go*."

He shoved her, and she hurried to get into position on the other side of the curtain again, clambering over Archie's body like he was a lump in the mattress. She heard the hiss of Apostolos's torch and then the stench of burning flesh. Their reluctant patient didn't wake this time.

For better or worse, it was done.

* * *

It was midnight, but neither could sleep. They'd pulled kitchen chairs over to Archie's bed and sat watching him while they sipped warm beer. Apostolos puffed on an acrid cigarette, but she didn't have the heart to ask him to put it out. She'd seen how his hands were trembling.

"Do you think he'll be okay?"

Flora barely recognized the voice as the captain's. She'd never heard him sound vulnerable before. She stared at Archie, who was so pale and silent it was as if he were already gone, and lied. "Yes, of course he will."

"I've never had to do anything like that. I've never cut a man, ever."

"You weren't cutting him; you were helping him. You tried to save his life. If he doesn't make it, it's the creature's fault, not yours."

He ran a hand through his unruly hair. "There was so much blood, Duchovney."

It had taken them over an hour to dispose of the bloody towels and sheets and wash away the evidence of their handiwork. *So much blood.* Not only Archie's, but Liam's. And George's. And Frank's. And poor Thor's. Every time they believed they'd seen the last of the violence, there had been more.

"He'll be okay," she said, and they fell silent again, watching the rise and fall of Archie's chest as he slept through the night.

Neither of them looked at his leg.

CHAPTER THIRTY-ONE

The darkness closed in on him. *I should have asked them to leave a light on.* Ordinarily, he would never have admitted being uncomfortable in the dark, but things had progressed far past ordinary.

At least the screaming had stopped—both from the radio and the tortured man. And the wail of the saw—he couldn't bear to consider what that particular sound meant. While it was happening, the shrieking combined with the music to create an unbearable cacophony, but the ship was silent now. Almost too quiet. The more Thor thought about the man and the way he had screamed, the more scared he got. *What if the creatures return? What if I'm the only one left?*

Flora.

He maneuvered himself into a sitting position, remembering all too well the penalty for moving fast. The collar of his shirt was caked with blood, but when he gingerly felt his head, he didn't find anything fresh. The pounding behind his temples had receded too, but whether from the aspirin or the sleep he didn't know.

The darkness of the cabin was disorienting. Had he slept for hours or days? He had no idea, but as he touched his feet to the floor, his stomach growled. He couldn't recall the last time he'd thought of food. The lunch he'd shared with Flora had taken place a lifetime ago.

As he crept down the passageway, he was relieved to see light spilling onto the floor from Frank's cabin. At least the electricity was working. The possibility of being trapped on this barge in perpetual darkness was more than he could bear.

The floorboards creaked under Thor's feet, and the planks moved in tandem with the ocean, swaying side to side. Leaning against the wall for balance, he shuffled the last few steps to Frank's room.

Someone was in the sailor's bed, a great mass huddled under a blanket, and for a moment, Thor was confused. *Had they brought Frank's body inside?* The thought disgusted him, but as he ventured closer, he realized the man was Archie. Or at least, it *had* been Archie.

The man's breath came in choking gasps, and Thor knew something wasn't right. He laid a hand on Archie's clammy forehead like a mother would. The man's skin was damp with sweat, but his temperature was normal. His color was horrible, though, as if he were dead already.

Guilt settled on Thor's shoulders like a lead blanket. He'd resented Archie for leaving him to deal with Frank alone, but now it was obvious he really had been ill. Thor wasn't sure what was wrong with him, but it wasn't as simple as the flu. He'd seen healthier-looking people in a morgue.

As he turned to go, Archie seized his hand, startling him. Thor's head pounded as he clung to the bunk to steady himself.

"They took my leg, Thor." Archie's voice was a wheeze. Tears spilled down his cheeks.

Thor was tempted to dismiss it as the ravings of a sick man, but Archie didn't seem delusional. "Who took your leg?"

"The Greek and Flora. They talked me into it." Archie panted between each word, growing more and more agitated as he fought to catch his breath. "But now I've changed my mind."

Thor couldn't believe it. This voyage was a nightmare that would never end. Why would Apostolos and Flora remove Archie's leg? The man's lower body was hidden by a blanket, but the shape created by his right leg did appear suspiciously short. Thor noticed rubber sheeting draped over the lower half of the bed. "What was wrong with you? Why were you sick?"

Archie tried to sit up but didn't quite make it, falling against the pillow with a series of raspy coughs. "It was the creature. Some of its—stuff—got on me. It was eating away my foot. But just my foot. Not this much. They took too much. Now I'm crippled. No one's ever going to hire me." He sobbed, hiding his face in his calloused hands.

Patting his shoulder awkwardly, Thor wondered how to comfort him. He'd been unconscious when the decision was made to amputate Archie's leg, and he couldn't say he was sorry about that. The screaming made sense now. He wondered how Flora had dealt with something so gory. Hopefully Apostolos had done most of the dirty work. "Someone will always hire you. You're a good man."

"But a man with one leg is not a man. Who's going to want me? How will I ever face Marie again, or the kids?"

He wept harder as Thor fumbled for the right words.

"Your wife and kids won't care, Archie. It's you they love, not your ugly leg."

Archie smiled a little at that, and wiped his tears on his sleeve. "Fuck you, Anderssen."

"I'll leave that to Marie." Thor was relieved Archie's despair had lightened somewhat, although he was sure it would return. Archie was accustomed to oilrig work, where being able bodied was a prerequisite. But there was not a doubt in Thor's mind that as long as Apostolos captained a ship, Archie would have a job.

"It hurts."

"I'm sure it does. Do you want some more aspirin?"

Archie managed a weak grin. "I think this calls for something a little stronger. Does the Greek have any more of that rum around? My head feels like it's going to split in two, but at least it'll help me get a few more hours sleep."

"I'll check."

Like the rest of the crew, Thor knew where their boss kept his stash, but none of them had ever dared touch it, no matter how sick they were of lukewarm beer. If Apostolos had shared his rum with Archie, he must have felt the situation was dire. Thor nudged a couple of empty bottles out of the way as he left the room. Frank's cabin looked like it had seen one hell of a party.

If only that were true.

* * *

The control room where Apostolos kept his rum was eerily quiet. Of course, the engine hadn't magically returned to life since Thor had been unconscious, but he wished it had.

He was grateful to find the cabinet under the window unlocked. There were two bottles of spiced rye standing sentry against the side, as if they were hiding, but the rum was gone. Thor grabbed a single bottle and then returned to get the other. It was going to take Archie a while to get over the worst of the pain.

"Beer isn't strong enough for you?"

Whirling around, his heart pounding, Thor saw a hulking shape in a chair in the corner. He exhaled in a rush. "Sorry, Captain. I assumed you were in bed."

"Apparently."

Apostolos was sarcastic but he didn't sound angry, or at least nowhere near as angry as Thor would have expected. "It's for Archie. He's awake, and he's in a lot of pain."

"We had to take his leg."

It was unnerving, talking to Apostolos without being able to see his face. For the second time that evening, Thor wished for light. "He told me. Was it the same thing Liam had?"

The captain sighed. "Looked like. I hope we got it in time."

"I'm sorry I wasn't able to help."

"I'm sorry I was. Be happy you weren't. Trust me, it wasn't anything you would have wanted to see."

"Is everything all right, Captain?" It wasn't like Apostolos to mope around in the dark.

"Do you believe in an honorable death, Anderssen?"

His question gave Thor chills. "What are you talking about?"

"Oh, Tomkins was babbling about it earlier, but I didn't pay much attention. Now I understand what he meant. Wouldn't you rather have a death of your own choosing than wait and be a victim of circumstance?"

Thor pulled a chair over to his boss, setting the rye on the floor. He still couldn't see much of him, but every now and then, the clouds would part and a glint of moonlight would catch Apostolos's eyes. "I'm well enough to fix the ship now, Captain. I just needed to rest for a bit. I can get us going in the morning."

"I always said you had a hard head, Anderssen. Who knew that would turn out to be such a blessing?"

Before Thor could think of a comeback, gravity returned to the captain's voice.

"I'm afraid it's too late for me. You'll have to run this barge yourself. I have no doubt you can do it. You always were the smartest guy on this ship. If you run into trouble, get Duchovney to help you. There's no moss growing on that brain of hers either."

"I don't understand. What are you saying?" Thor gripped the arms of his chair. There was a resignation in the Greek's voice he'd never heard before.

"Watch your eyes." There was a click, and light from the battery-powered lantern on the captain's desk shone in Thor's face. Once his eyes had adjusted, he longed for blindness.

Tiny blisters covered Apostolos's features. Or at least Thor thought they were blisters at first. But even before the heartbreaking truth dawned on him, he could tell it wasn't that simple. The sores were alive, growing and opening and oozing as he watched. He dropped his gaze and heard another click as the Greek shut off the light.

"You can see why I'm sitting in the dark."

"But how—?"

"When I removed Tomkins's leg, I must have gotten splashed. I tried to be careful, but it was…messy."

Seeing Apostolos's face had been horrible, but sitting in the dark with him, knowing what was happening, was worse. Thor could hear the faint sizzling of the captain's skin being consumed, and remembered Liam screaming in the shower.

Thor cleared his throat. "Does Flora know?"

"No. She went to bed before it started. The first one was on my hand." Apostolos's voice cracked. "I told myself it was just a boil, but then my face began to burn. It's good she doesn't see this. The fewer people who have contact with me, the better. It's too easy for whatever this is to spread."

"We're not going to desert you, Captain. There has to be a way."

Apostolos laughed. "Are you crazy? Did that knock on the head take away your sense? Would you like another look? I'm not going to sit here while all my skin dissolves. That's not an honorable death." He shifted in his seat, his open wounds squelching. "To be honest with you, I'm fucking terrified."

The idea of the Greek leaving them without a rudder made Thor feel helpless and desperate, but he couldn't argue. There was no point. At the rate the sores were growing, whatever was left of his face would be a bloody mess by morning.

"What are you going to do?"

Apostolos shifted again. Thor could tell he was toying with something, but he couldn't see what it was. He didn't need to.

"That's been taken care of. If all goes well, I'll fall over the bow, but if not, you're going to have to push me over afterward. Don't let Duchovney see. And don't get anywhere near me with bare skin. Make sure you're covered."

Thor nodded, forgetting the captain couldn't see him. "When?"

"At first light, I reckon. I want to see the sun rise."

"We have time then." He pushed himself from the chair, ignoring the pain that shot through his head.

"Time for what?"

"For you to show me everything there is to know about running this ship. And once you've shown me, I'm going to teach Flora."

Thor expected him to argue, but the captain got to his feet, leading the way to the controls. "Just don't get too close. And for the love of God, don't touch me. You're going to make it out of here, Anderssen."

How he wished he could believe that.

CHAPTER THIRTY-TWO

When Flora shuffled into the messdeck at seven in the morning, Thor was slumped over a cup of coffee like he'd already been there for hours.

"Good morning."

He lifted his head, squinting at her. "Morning."

"How are you feeling?" Any optimism she'd had when she'd first woken had vanished when she'd seen him. He'd managed to clean himself up, but he still looked terrible, even though he was wearing a new shirt, and his skin and hair were no longer caked with dried blood.

"I'm okay." He curved his lips in a weak smile that didn't meet his eyes. "How are you? I gather I missed some excitement yesterday."

Flora grimaced, shaking her head. "If I learned anything yesterday, it's that I have nothing to complain about. He's improving, though—don't you think?"

"Yeah, I think so. You guys did the right thing."

She poked around in the cooler.

"There's bread left if you want toast," Thor said. "But no eggs. I think we still have canned milk, and there's plenty of cereal."

She settled for dry toast. The thought of the canned milk, warm and sweet smelling, made her stomach churn. "If I get home, one of the first things I'm going to do—after I hug my son nearly to death—is go out for breakfast."

"You *will* get home, Flora. I'm going to fix the ship today, but before I do, I'm going to teach you how to run it."

Her eyes widened. She couldn't believe what he was saying. Why was every man on this ship determined to commit suicide? "You can't try it again yet. You're not ready."

"Yes I am. In any case, we have no choice. We're running out of time. We have a deadline, remember?"

He looked worn out and sad, the dark circles under his eyes adding at least ten years to his age. Flora reached out with her mind. "They're not around. Or at least, they're not close. I think they've decided to give us some room to do what we need."

"How long do you think that will last?" Thor ran a hand over his stubble and rubbed his temples, wincing.

"They're unpredictable. We can't count on them, so we have to count on ourselves. Have you talked to Apostolos about this?" Flora assumed the Greek would agree with her. Thor was in no shape to go in the water again.

"Yeah. He thinks we should get the hell out of here as soon as possible, so let's hope you're a quick study."

Flora had seen him twitch when she said the Greek's name. "Where is he? I'd like to talk to him myself."

"He's gone, Flora."

His voice dropped so low she had to strain to hear it. She could feel every muscle in her body tense. *No. Please no. Not Apostolos.* "What do you mean, he's gone?"

"When he was—*helping* Archie, his face got splashed. He wouldn't want you to mourn him. He chose to die with honor. At least he got to see the sun rise one last time."

Tears ran down her cheeks. "Were you there?"

"No, he asked me not to be. I left him alone, and when I came on deck later, he was gone." He leaned over and touched her shoulder. "It was the right thing to do, Flora. It was what he wanted. I saw his wounds, and he wouldn't have survived the day."

She drew deep breaths through clenched teeth, fighting to keep from sobbing. "What are we going to do? He was the only one who knew how to run this thing."

"Not anymore. He taught me, and I'm going to teach you. Just in case."

As Thor walked past her, she caught his hand in hers. It was soft as a boy's. He wasn't old enough to have developed any calluses, and the thought made her want to weep. She couldn't imagine what it would be like to stand in front of his mother, breaking the news that her son would never be coming home.

"There can't be any 'in case,' Thor. I don't want you to take the risk. You're not well enough."

His hand tightened around hers, helping her to her feet. "I'm fine. Like Apostolos says, I have a hard head. He had a lot of respect for you, Flora, and so do I. Archie and me, we need your help."

During her marine biology days, she'd been at the helm of many boats, but never a ship of this magnitude. Still, the mechanics of it were the least of her worries. All their preparations would be for nothing if Thor couldn't get the boat fixed.

* * *

"Thank you."

She was startled to see Archie sitting in bed, grinning at her. "You're *thanking* me?"

"Sure, and why not? You saved my life, you and the captain. I'm not sure I would have had the guts to do what you did if the shoe was on the other foot."

Her mind still reeled with the news of Apostolos's death, but she forced herself to laugh at Archie's bad pun. She decided not to tell him about the Greek, unless he painted her into a corner. "How's the leg?"

"Itchy as hell." He hooked his fingers into claws, pawing the air. "I'm tempted to tear it off myself."

"That's good, though. It means it's healing," she said with more confidence than she felt. She was sure she'd read that somewhere. She hoped it was true. "Can I take a look?"

"Better you than me."

Peeling off the blankets, she was relieved when she saw the bandage she'd applied that morning was white and clean. Above the stump, there were no blisters or other sores. She covered the leg again, overwhelmed with gratitude.

"What's the verdict, Doc? Will I live?"

She smiled. "For now. Can I get you anything? Are you hungry?"

"Thor brought me a sandwich a little while ago, but I'd love some more aspirin. And some water."

Flora dropped the white pills into his cupped palm and handed him a bottle of water. She'd never suspected Frank would bring her anything but grief, but he was the only one who had thought to bring so many painkillers.

"Thanks," he said. "I can't see them helping much, but I figure it beats nothing."

"I wish we had something stronger. I guess we'll know for next time."

He gave her a funny look. "Do you really think there will be a next time?"

She laughed. "No, I guess not."

"So where is our Mr. Anderssen? Did you put him to work somewhere?"

"No, he's napping, thankfully. I don't think he got any sleep last night." Flora was worried Thor might have a concussion, but it didn't much matter. If he did, there wasn't anything she could do for him.

"I'm not surprised. I wasn't exactly quiet." Archie's face reddened.

She squeezed his hand. "You were amazing. You're a survivor, Archie. Thor is going to fix this ship tonight, and then you're going to go home to see Marie and your kids. How does that sound?"

"It sounds like a dream."

"You should get some rest now. The more healing time you can give that leg, the more you'll improve your chances."

She was almost at the door before he stopped her. "Apostolos left, didn't he?"

Flora dreaded seeing her sadness mirrored on Archie's face, but she wasn't about to lie to him. "Yes, this morning. After sunrise."

Archie nodded. "That's what he told me he would do. The man always did believe in keeping his word. He came to say goodbye to me, you know."

"I wish he'd said goodbye to me." More tears fell before she could stop them.

"I don't think he wanted you to see him that way. He already"—Archie swallowed hard—"didn't look like himself."

"I could have handled it."

"It wasn't a matter of whether or not you could handle it. He wanted to protect you. No matter what, we were his crew, and the man always took care of his crew."

"Then why did he come to see you?"

"He said he had to apologize. He felt bad about my leg, he said, and hoped I could forgive him. I told him he'd done nothing to be forgiven for." He shook his head. "Apologizing for saving my life. Wasn't that just like him?"

Flora remembered the man she'd once resented and feared in equal measure. No matter how bleak things were, the Greek had never failed to do what needed to be done.

She resolved to tell the world what kind of man he'd been. She only hoped she'd get the chance.

"Yes," she said. "That was just like him."

CHAPTER THIRTY-THREE

"Are you sure there's nothing I can say to change your mind?"

Thor would have laughed if his head weren't in danger of cracking open. "Like I'd tell you if there was." Tugging at the wetsuit, he pulled it over his stomach, chest, and shoulders. It wasn't as much of a struggle as it used to be. He turned so Flora could zip him up. "If you're this good at nagging now, by the time Zach's a teenager, you'll have driven him crazy."

He'd meant it as a joke, but her face fell and he cursed his big mouth. "I'm sorry, Flora. That was tasteless. I know how much you miss him."

"It's not that. I don't mean to be a nag, but what if something happens to you? We need you."

Her dark eyes dominated her pale face, which had become more angular with each passing week. Thor wasn't the only one who had dropped a few pounds. "But you don't. You now know as much about running this ship as I do." As Apostolos had predicted, she hadn't had any trouble mastering the controls.

She snorted, but he could see from her smile that the compliment pleased her. "Hardly."

"I saw Archie, and he looks great—much better than I expected. But you know as well as I do he's going to need more than aspirin to get through this. I can't put this off any longer. Believe me, if I thought there was another option, I would take it."

"One more day wouldn't make a difference," she said in that stubborn way of hers, but he could see the mention of Archie had swayed her a little.

"Are you willing to bet his life on it?" Knowing what her answer would be, Thor walked to the side of the ship and lowered himself onto the metal ladder. Lingering a moment, he held on to the top rung, not quite ready to let go.

"Be careful," she said, and he nodded, admiring the midday sun caught in her hair, the dark curls gleaming with gold.

"How's your friend?" The memory of what lurked beneath gave Thor the creeps. After this, he wouldn't venture near the ocean for a long, long time—if ever.

"Keeping his distance, as promised."

He wanted to ask if she thought the creature was trustworthy, but knew there was no point. They *had* to trust it, whether or not that was the wisest course of action.

Flora leaned over the side and wrapped her arms around his shoulders in an awkward hug. "Take care of yourself."

"This isn't goodbye. I have no intention of dying down there." Still, his voice was shaky. He returned her embrace as best he could with one arm, patting her on the back. "Well, this isn't going to get any easier. I'm off."

He concentrated on the ladder for the rest of the way down, afraid to see the concern in her eyes. Out of everyone, she had the closest link to the creature, so why was she worried? His focus had to be on the ship, so he pushed the fear out of his mind and slipped into the crystal-clear waters.

It took a special kind of insanity to fix a boat while it was still in the water, but he'd always liked the challenge. He could easily imagine himself in space, tinkering with the ISS in zero gravity.

A few curious tropical fish—mostly striped sergeant majors and French grunts—flittered about his legs and facemask, not scared in the least by the breathing tube. He waved them away so he could concentrate. Within ten minutes, he'd repaired the damaged cable, and his heart slowed to its normal rhythm.

The leak was a different story, but he'd spent many hours lying in bed visualizing it over the last couple of days. He was confident he could repair it without having to break for another oxygen tank. Thor climbed high enough on the ladder to give Flora an update.

"How's it going down there?"

"So far, so good. The cable's fixed, but that was the easy part. Let's hope the same goes for the leak."

"Maybe—maybe you should leave that for another day."

He sighed, sounding more exasperated than he meant to. "We talked about this before. We don't have time. Archie could take a turn for the worse at any moment."

"I know. I'm sorry. I don't mean to sound like a broken record. It's just—well, it'll sound silly, but I have a bad feeling."

Hesitating on the ladder, he felt his heart kick into second gear again. "Is it your friend?"

"No, all's quiet there. This is something else. Or it might be nothing. Maybe I'm paranoid, but I'm not feeling good about this. It would be great if you could finish tomorrow morning."

"We have no idea what the weather conditions will be like tomorrow. This is perfect—you couldn't ask for a calmer day. I've been thinking about that leak a lot, and I think I could have it repaired in ten minutes. Just ten minutes, Flora."

Reaching forward, he squeezed her hand with his glove, which was damp with seawater. She didn't pull away. "Are you with me?" he asked. "Only ten minutes."

"If you see that it's going to take longer, will you come in?"

He considered her request. More than anything, he wanted to get the job done when the waters were calm. Repairing the leak would be impossible in a rough sea. But he agreed. Maybe it *was* paranoia, but it didn't take a genius to see Flora was genuinely scared. It was worth waiting a few hours if it set her mind at ease.

"Please be careful, Thor." She leaned her head over the side to watch him as he slipped into the water.

He grinned at her before inserting the respirator. "You worry too much."

CHAPTER THIRTY-FOUR

Waking from my mid-afternoon nap, I felt more relaxed than I had since this nightmare began. Everything was peaceful in the lair for a change. If this was the price we had to pay for denying our son, it was more than worth it. Perhaps we should punish him more often, but only if he agreed to give us the silent treatment again.

Ah, bliss. Sweet bliss.

Gliding out of the den I shared with my wife, I was startled to find her in the main part of our lair. This area of our home featured the most brightly colored coral and was where we entertained. It was also where the humans' drill had broken through, but nature had swiftly repaired the puncture as existing plant life grew to fill the space. You couldn't even see the damage now. I was pleased we'd been able to protect our reef.

"Good afternoon, dearheart."

She regarded me, her face slack with boredom. "How was your nap?"

"Most refreshing, thank you. I'm surprised to find you here alone. Did you eat?"

"A little. Mostly what drifted by." She scowled. "I'm not that hungry."

This was cause for concern. I couldn't recall the last time my wife had lost her appetite.

"Where's The Boy?" I asked, looking around. I realized that our lair was indeed peaceful—*too* peaceful, even with my son sulking and my wife disgruntled.

My wife flicked her tail. "I haven't seen him yet today."

"This is getting ridiculous. I'll go talk to him."

"You'll only make him angrier."

"That's not my intention, but letting it pass isn't doing us any good. He'll hold this grudge until the next millennium."

Before she could argue, I rushed to my son's cave with fear growing in my gut. Spoiled, spoiled child. How dare he do this to his mother?

I barged into his filthy den, fully expecting to find him there, lounging about with that pouty expression that had become all too familiar lately.

It took a minute for it to register that he wasn't in the room.

The cave was empty.

A second later, a razor-edged scream pierced my brain.

CHAPTER THIRTY-FIVE

Flora scanned the ocean. No matter how many deep breaths she took, she couldn't quiet her nerves. There was something wrong, but what? Frustrated, she shook her head to clear it. The ocean gave her no answers. It was calm—perhaps too calm. When was the last time she'd seen a dolphin, or a whale? Even the schools of tiny fish that clustered near the ship hoping for handouts were absent today.

She let her mind wander into the ocean to the depths below. There was no response, no sensation that anything had received her signal. Dread leaned on her shoulders, making it hard to breathe. She knew it was in her head—she was nervous about being alone on the ship; that was all.

But if she'd learned anything this past month, it was to trust her instincts.

Something burst out of the water.

She opened her mouth to scream, but it was only Thor, grinning around the respirator. He spit it out of his mouth and reached for the ladder. Rivulets of salt water streamed off his wet suit, giving him the sleek look of a seal. "It's fixed," he told her, as if his triumphant expression hadn't already communicated the news. "At least, I think so. Just need to make sure the engine hasn't been damaged, and then we'll start her. Give it a try."

Seeing her expression, he groaned. "What's the problem? Did you get another message from your friend?"

"No, and that's the problem. Everything's too quiet. Haven't you noticed? Even the fish are gone." Her words tumbled over one another. She inhaled deeply, telling herself to calm down. Men did not respond well to panic, especially from women. They tended to write it off as hysterics. "I've been standing here, trying my best to convince myself this is in my head. But it isn't, Thor. I've got a really bad feeling, and I think you should leave everything how it is for now. The leak is fixed, right?"

"Yeah, but the propellers are coated with gunk. It'll take a minute for me to clean them. Easily ten minutes, twenty tops." When she stayed silent, he sighed. "Come on, Flora. Don't you want to go home?"

"Of course I do." The words sounded angrier than she'd meant. "But I want *both* of us to go home. I'm afraid that if you go down there again, you're not going to come back."

"That's what you said this morning, and yet I'm here, aren't I?" His tone was teasing, and she nearly screamed with frustration.

"You also said it would take you ten minutes to fix the leak." She'd been standing on the deck for at least half an hour, her heart in her throat. She'd felt every one of those minutes, and had aged accordingly.

"Sorry, Mom. Took longer than I thought." He rolled his eyes, giving her a view of what Zach would become in another ten years.

Infuriated, she shoved his chest with such force that he nearly toppled off the ladder. His eyes widened. "Easy."

"Go ahead and kill yourself, then. I should have known you wouldn't listen to me. None of you ever did, and look where it got you. I thought things would be different now."

"Hey, that's not fair. I always listened to you. You know that," he said, sounding hurt. "I need to finish this, Flora. Archie doesn't have much time. This isn't just about us."

"Archie would agree with me," she said with conviction, though she wasn't sure. Men tended to stick together.

"What difference is ten minutes going to make?"

"I don't know. I told you—I don't know what's wrong. I only know that something is."

"But what if you have that feeling again tonight? And tomorrow? And the week after that? What if a storm comes tomorrow?"

"Fine, go. You obviously have your mind made up." She turned away from him, overwhelmed with sadness as she heard his flippers squeak on the metal ladder and his mask snap as he fitted it into place. Flora rushed to the side of the ship, wanting to plead with him one more time.

But it was too late.

All she saw was his hair, darkened from the water, swirling around his head as he plunged into the ocean.

CHAPTER THIRTY-SIX

Damn that woman. Damn her and her intuition.

Flora had gotten to him more than he liked to admit. She always did. And she was wrong about his not believing her. He'd listened to her from the very start, even when the other guys had mocked and taunted her. It bothered him that she didn't recognize that. He'd have to talk to her that night, maybe after dinner. By then, she'd hopefully be in a better mood.

The thing to do now was finish cleaning the propellers. Everything else could wait.

Flora was right about the fish. They normally clustered around him as soon as he set foot in the water, but he couldn't see a single one. Maybe a storm was coming.

The sensation something was watching him grew stronger. His pulse quickened.

Steady, Anderssen. Don't be an idiot. You're almost done.

His growing unease—and the urge to turn around to see what was causing it—was almost unbearable. His skin tightened along his spine until it felt like it didn't quite fit. Squinting through the bubbles of his respirator, he brushed away the flakes of rust. *Good enough. It will get us home.* The company could worry about the damage.

He swam around the hull of the ship, staying close enough that barnacles caught one of his gloves and tore it open, scratching the skin beneath.

As a plume of blood flowed into the water from his injured finger, he knew the situation wasn't good. Sharks could smell blood from an incredible distance, even miniscule amounts. He used his legs to propel him through the water, increasing his speed.

Thor heard something behind him. Turning his head, he saw something rushing toward him. It wasn't a shark. He wasn't sure what it was—some brownish-green horror with a face like a nightmare. Its jaws closed around his throat before he could scream.

CHAPTER THIRTY-SEVEN

I reached the ship as my son bit off the young mechanic's head. As the man's blood flooded the water, the geologist's cries threatened to crush my brain. My wife shrieked too. Both women directed their anguish at me, but only my wife's thoughts were decipherable.

Don't hurt him.

There wasn't time to consider what she meant before our son turned to me, gloating in the kill, his eyes half-mad with bloodlust. Part of the young man's arm hung from his jaws, and I winced as he swallowed.

Don't tempt me, kid.

Draugen slipped behind me, but for once, I wasn't afraid. I'd told The Boy again and again to stay away from the ship and the humans, but he didn't listen.

He never did.

The woman was still screaming. I didn't blame her this time. After all, I'd promised that her friend would be fine. I'd betrayed her. My *family* had betrayed her.

My son reared his head at me, flaunting his ugly neck in an attempt to make himself look bigger. I'd never been so disgusted, so ashamed of him, as I was then. He chewed on bits of the engineer, his acidic saliva doing the rest of the work, dissolving the scraps of flesh. Shreds of neoprene floated around us. In his bloodlust, my son ate some of those too.

"Go away, Father. This is none of your business. This is *my* ship. Mom promised me."

"Let him go."

A leg with a flipper attached disappeared down The Boy's gullet. My son snarled at me, using words that should never be directed at one's elders.

Whipping my tail around, I struck him across the chest. Black blood gushed from a dozen different wounds, and my son cried out in pain. Finally sensing the danger he was in, he moved away from the ship, swimming as well as he was able. My wife's teeth closed around one of my fins, but I shook her off, growling. This should have been done long ago—I would not be responsible for bringing a monster into the world.

Before I went after him, I searched the now-murky water. The young man's head was intact, his poor mouth agape in a scream of horror. A foggy mask hid his eyes, which I suspected was a blessing.

I didn't know if seeing his face again would give the geologist comfort or a bigger shock, but I seized it by the hair and lofted it onto the ship's deck as carefully as I could.

I'm sorry. I cannot change what happened to your friend, but I swear to you my son will pay for this.

Had the young man been her friend? I wasn't sure. She had some motherly instincts toward him, almost as if they were family.

Almost as if he had been her son.

Perhaps that's just the way females are.

My own son hadn't gotten far. It was easy to catch him. When he saw me coming after him, the terror in his eyes was gratifying—he was finally giving me the respect I'd always wanted. Always wanted, but never gotten. Shame it had to come to this.

Strengthening my resolve, I pursued him with a roar that reverberated through the ocean. I knew the woman would hear it—creatures from worlds away would hear it. My wife rushed to attack, as I expected. It was her duty to protect her son, no matter what kind of despicable hell spawn he was.

My tail ripped a hole in his side. Instead of fleeing, he lunged at my face, baring his fangs. A new burst of fury consumed me. Closing my jaws around his scaly neck, I bit down. It would be over soon.

Don't, Nøkken. He's our only child. Our kind will die out, my wife pleaded.

How could I explain what had to be done? In spite of our best efforts, our son resisted every attempt to mold him into a merciful creature. As he grew to full power, nothing would be safe—not our fellow marine life, and maybe not even us.

Even if Draugen killed me right then, which she surely could, my death throes would only make me bite down harder.

Either way, it was finished.

I snapped my teeth together, severing my son's head from his neck, exactly like he'd done to the unfortunate mechanic.

My wife screamed again, but this time in rage. She came after me with murder in her heart, and I suspected she'd wanted to for a while. No matter how we try to suppress our true nature, it is always there, lurking, waiting for us. It's in our blood.

As I steeled myself for the last battle, I spared one more thought for the human.

Start your little boat and get far away from here. I won't be able to distract her for long.

I only hoped this time she would follow my advice.

CHAPTER THIRTY-EIGHT

Flora clung to the deck, which bucked and rolled underneath her as the immense creatures fought it out below.

Cradling Thor's head in a towel, she hurried downstairs, blinking away the tears that stung her eyes. There was no time to get emotional. Archie was still alive, and she had to get him away from here. Far away.

"Flora."

She could hear him calling now, as he'd probably been calling since Thor was attacked. Yes, *attacked.* A violent word, but vague enough for her purposes. That's how she would choose to remember what happened. She would not let her mind stray to the terrible way he'd died.

Was it her imagination, or did Archie sound weaker? The thought made her knees buckle. *Not now. Not after everything.*

"It's okay. Thor fixed the ship. I'm going to start the engine, and then I'll be in to see you." *Please, God, let it start.*

She was terrified he would ask why Thor wasn't taking the helm, but perhaps he already knew.

"Okay," he yelled back. A series of racking coughs followed. He didn't sound good.

Hurrying to the control room, Flora started the ship the way Thor had shown her. When it sputtered and died, she struck her fist against the console in spite of her resolve to stay calm.

We're dead; it was all for nothing.

Then the engine caught. The lights on the control board flickered to weary life as she plugged in the coordinates Apostolos had scribbled down. For the first time in days, the ship began to move, an old woman rising from her wheelchair.

"Thank you, Thor," she whispered. "You did it."

There was every reason to worry the repair wouldn't hold, or that the fuel would run out before they reached home, but she knew Thor would want her to be optimistic. She owed him that much. Her only job was to keep Archie alive. Just for a few more days.

She stood at the helm, mesmerized at the sight of the prow cutting its way through teal water. There was a beauty about it, even to the slight tilt under her feet that made her feel like she would topple over at any moment. It had been too many days since she'd needed her sea legs.

Tearing her attention from the view, she headed to the messdeck with the cherished bundle tucked under her arm. Even though she'd tenderly dried Thor's face and hair after rinsing away the salt water, he was still damp when she placed him in the freezer. Flora hoped he would forgive her.

It was no way to treat a friend, but she was doing her best.

She knew he would respect that.

ABOUT THE AUTHOR

Raised in the far north, amid Jack London's world of dog sleds and dark winters, J.H. Moncrieff has been a professional writer all of her adult life.

Harlequin recently conducted a worldwide search for "the next Gillian Flynn" to launch their new line of psychological thrillers, and Moncrieff was one of two authors selected. Her novella, The Bear Who Wouldn't Leave, was featured in Samhain's Childhood Fears collection and stayed on their horror bestsellers list for over a year.

During her years as a journalist, she tracked down snipers and canoed through crocodile-infested waters. She has published hundreds of articles in national and international magazines and newspapers.

When she's not writing, she loves to travel to exotic locations, advocate for animal rights, and muay thai kickbox.

J.H. loves to hear from readers and fellow writers. You can email her at jh@jhmoncrieff.com, or connect with her on Facebook: www.facebook.com/jhmoncrieff and Twitter: www.twitter.com/JH_Moncrieff.

Visit her website at www.jhmoncrieff.com.

ACKNOWLEDGMENTS

Many thanks to Steve Bornstein for generously sharing his experiences working in offshore drilling with me, and to Rhonda Parrish for connecting us. I've had to take some creative license when it came to The Cormorant, so any errors are mine, not Steve's.

The folks at Severed Press have been great to work with, and I'm thrilled to be one of their authors.

Being a writer is wonderful, but it can also be isolating. I'm lucky to have a tremendous support system, especially my copy editor and spouse Chris Brogden, Dee-Dee Gould and Drew Kozub from my writing group, my personal cheerleaders Christine Brandt, Anita Siraki, Nikki Burch, Kay Deveroux, Brenda Furst, Maxine Brogden, and Lisa Saunders, and all of my blog readers, friends, and my parents for their years of encouragement. The horror writing community has been incredibly welcoming and supportive, in particular Don D'Auria, Mercedes M. Yardley, Hunter Shea, Chuck Wendig, Ronald Malfi, Theresa Braun, Catherine Cavendish, JG Faherty, Brian Kirk, Somer Canon, Jonathan Moore, Tausha Johnson, Brian Moreland, and Russell R. James.

I'm truly blessed to be surrounded by such talented people. I'd like to also recognize and thank the people of Standing Rock for sacrificing so much to protect their water and environment. Stay strong.

CHECK OUT OTHER GREAT
DEEP SEA THRILLERS

MEGATOOTH
by Viktor Zarkov

When the death rate of sperm whales rises dramatically, a well-respected environmental activist puts together a ragtag team to hit the high seas to investigate the matter. They suspect that the deaths are due to poachers and they are all driven by a need for justice.

Elsewhere, an experimental government vessel is enhancing deep sea mining equipment. They see one of these dead whales up close and personal...and are fairly certain that it wasn't poachers that killed it.

Both of these teams are about to discover that poachers are the least of their worries. There is something hunting the whales...

Something big
Something prehistoric.
Something terrifying.
MEGATOOTH!

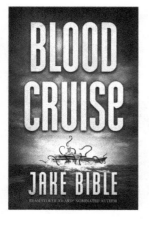

BLOOD CRUISE
by Jake Bible

Ben Clow's plans are set. Drop off kids, pick up girlfriend, head to the marina, and hop on best friend's cruiser for a weekend of fun at sea. But Ben's happy plans are about to be changed by a tentacled horror that lurks beneath the waves.

International crime lords! Deep cover black ops agents! A ravenous, bloodsucking monster! A storm of evil and danger conspire to turn Ben Clow's vacation from a fun ocean getaway into a nightmare of a Blood Cruise!

CHECK OUT OTHER GREAT DEEP SEA THRILLERS

SEA RAPTOR
by John J. Rust

From terrorist hunter to monster hunter! Jack Rastun was a decorated U.S. Army Ranger, until an unfortunate incident forced him out of the service. He is soon hired by the Foundation for Undocumented Biological Investigation and given a new mission, to search for cryptids, creatures whose existence has not been proven by mainstream science. Teaming up with the daring and beautiful wildlife photographer Karen Thatcher, they must stop a sea monster's deadly rampage along the Jersey Shore. But that's not the only danger Rastun faces. A group of murderous animal smugglers also want the creature. Rastun must utilize every skill learned from years of fighting, otherwise, his first mission for the FUBI might very well be his last.

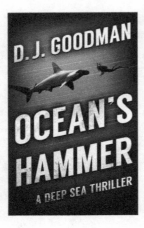

OCEAN'S HAMMER
by D.J. Goodman

Something strange is happening in the Sea of Cortez. Whales are beaching for no apparent reason and the local hammerhead shark population, previously believed to be fished to extinction, has suddenly reappeared. Marine biologists Maria Quintero and Kevin Hoyt have come to investigate with a television producer in tow, hoping to get footage that will land them a reality TV show. The plan is to have a stand-off against a notorious illegal shark-fishing captain and then go home.

Things are not going according to plan.

There is something new in the waters of the Sea of Cortez. Something smart. Something huge. Something that has its own plans for Quintero and Hoyt.

CHECK OUT OTHER GREAT DEEP SEA THRILLERS

THEY RISE
by Hunter Shea

Some call them ghost sharks, the oldest and strangest looking creatures in the sea.

Marine biologist Brad Whitley has studied chimaera fish all his life. He thought he knew everything about them. He was wrong. Warming ocean temperatures free legions of prehistoric chimaera fish from their methane ice suspended animation. Now, in a corner of the Bermuda Triangle, the ocean waters run red. The 400 million year old massive killing machines know no mercy, destroying everything in their path. It will take Whitley, his climatologist ex-wife and the entire US Navy to stop them in the bloodiest battle ever seen on the high seas.

SERPENTINE
by Barry Napier

Clarkton Lake is a picturesque vacation spot located in rural Virginia, great for fishing, skiing, and wasting summer days away.

But this summer, something is different. When butchered bodies are discovered in the water and along the muddy banks of Clarkton Lake, what starts out as a typical summer on the lake quickly turns into a nightmare.

This summer, something new lives in the lake...something that was born in the darkest depths of the ocean and accidentally brought to these typically peaceful waters.

It's getting bigger, it's getting smarter...and it's always hungry.

CPSIA information can be obtained
at www.ICGtesting.com
Printed in the USA
LVHW091420170520
655860LV00001B/285